D1443399

The Case of
the Wiggling Wig

The Case of
the Wiggling Wig

A McGurk Mystery

by E. W. Hildick

F
HIL

SIMON & SCHUSTER
BOOKS FOR YOUNG READERS

SIMON & SCHUSTER BOOKS FOR YOUNG READERS
An imprint of Simon & Schuster Children's Publishing Division
1230 Avenue of the Americas, New York, New York 10020
Copyright © 1996 by E. W. Hildick
All rights reserved including the right of reproduction
in whole or in part in any form.
SIMON & SCHUSTER BOOKS FOR YOUNG READERS is a trademark of Simon & Schuster.
Book design by Claudia Carlson
The text of this book is set in New Caledonia.
Printed and bound in the United States of America
First Edition
1 3 5 7 9 10 8 6 4 2

Library of Congress Cataloging-in-Publication Data
Hildick, E. W. (Edmund William), 1925–
The case of the wiggling wig: a McGurk mystery / by E. W. Hildick. — 1st ed.
p. cm.
Summary: McGurk is confined to an upstairs bedroom when he breaks his leg,
but that doesn't stop him and the rest of his detective organization from
uncovering a clever robbery scheme being plotted right next door.
[1. Mystery and detective stories.] I. Title.
PZ7.H5463Cavr 1996 [Fic]—dc20 95-25819 CIP AC
ISBN: 0-689-80087-7

13469

Contents

1

McGurk Goes Missing

Just what had happened to McGurk? Had he been attacked? Kidnapped? Killed?

These were the questions we were faced with that bright sunny morning in August.

There we'd been in his backyard, all unsuspecting, gathered outside the door to our basement headquarters. It had been weeks since the McGurk Organization had had a case and soon it would be back-to-school time again.

Then—wham!—*The Case of the Lost Leader*.

I, Joey Rockaway, the Organization's word expert and record keeper, never expected to be recording something like *that*.

Neither did any of the others.

When Wanda Grieg tried the door all she said was, "Huh! Locked! It looks like he's late."

"Maybe he has simply forgotten to unlock the door," said Mari Yoshimura.

"We'll soon see," said Wanda, knocking on the glass panel. "Open up, McGurk!"

Dead silence.

"I don't think he's even switched the light on yet," I said, going down the five steps and squeezing past Wanda.

It was difficult to tell. The glass was almost covered by the sign taped to the inside.

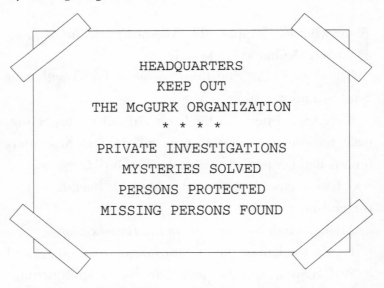

```
            HEADQUARTERS
             KEEP OUT
     THE McGURK ORGANIZATION
              * * * *
     PRIVATE INVESTIGATIONS
        MYSTERIES SOLVED
       PERSONS PROTECTED
    MISSING PERSONS FOUND
```

Which was only the beginning. There was a whole raft of extra pieces taped below it, describing other kinds of cases we'd handled.

"No." I peered closer, around the edges of the sign. "It's still in darkness."

"Well come on, then!" said Brains Bellingham. "Let's go lean on the front doorbell."

"Yeah!" said Willie Sandowsky. "Maybe he's still in *bed*!"

Being the longest legged as well as the longest nosed,

Willie beat us all to the front door and began pressing the bell.

"Hey, take it easy, Willie!" said Wanda. "We don't want to startle his *mom* out of her skin!"

But no one was being startled out of anything.

Just dead silence again, once Willie had taken his thumb off that bell.

"Looks like there's nobody home," he said, suddenly looking uneasy.

"Hey, the *garage!*" I said.

We'd already passed it, with its doors wide open and neither of the two cars inside. Mr. McGurk goes off early to work, and Mrs. McGurk might have slipped out to the shopping plaza. But to leave the deserted garage exposed was unusual.

In that house it was, anyway. I could just hear McGurk saying, "Okay, Mom, so you want to advertise to every passing opportunist thief, 'Hey, come on in, fella! Help yourself!'"

Then Brains noticed that a stack of plant pots just inside had been shaved and a couple knocked over and broken. And Wanda followed this up by spotting deep tire tracks in the gravel, where Mrs. McGurk's car must have accelerated immediately.

"My brother Ed's always doing that, but not Mrs. McGurk, surely? Not unless there's been some terrible emergency!"

This had us all dashing back to the basement door.

This time, as our eyes got more used to the dimness, we began to see things we'd not made out before.

My own discovery was kind of negative. McGurk's rocking chair at the battered round table looked uncannily still. "Nobody's been sitting in his chair in the last few minutes."

(It had occurred to me that he might have been testing us. Lying low—or *sitting* low—waiting to see how we'd handle the situation.)

But the others were way ahead of me.

"Two of *our* chairs have been overturned!" said Mari.

"Yes—and isn't that a pair of kitchen steps lying across them?" said Brains.

"And what *is* that?" said Wanda. "Glittering and glistening on the table? Broken *glass*?" Then she gasped. "And *that*? At the edge? Sort of spilling over, slowly, drop by drop. Coffee?"

By now, Willie had switched his attention to the cracks around the door itself, closing his eyes and using his sensitive nose instead.

"Coffee nothing!" He looked up at us, his eyes wide. "What I smell is *blood*!"

We stared at him in totally frozen horror. Then:

"Looking for Jack McGurk?" said a man's voice.

We all nearly jumped out of our skin then.

But it was only Mr. Jones, one of the neighbors.

"Whu-what happened?" I stammered.

"I don't know exactly. Except he was rushed off in an

ambulance about half an hour ago, with his mom high-tailing it after them in her car."

"It was that serious, huh?" said Wanda, in a hushed voice.

"Sure looked like it."

Well, that was better than McGurk having been kidnapped or murdered. But it was still a mystery.

So we began peering through those cracks again, and this time McGurk would have been really proud of us. I mean, although we were still shocked and horrified, we began to use our detective skills.

"It looks like he had placed the steps on the table and was standing on them when they slipped," said Mari.

"Or maybe he had put them on one of the chairs at the side," said Wanda. "And they slipped off that."

"Yeah! That glass," said Brains. "Look, it's from the ceiling light."

Sure enough, the glass cover had been removed.

"Replacing a bulb, maybe," I said.

"Hey! Maybe he's been electrocuted!" gasped Willie. *"Fried in his own HQ!"*

Wanda gulped. "It—it can't be as bad as *that*, Willie—can it? Surely you'd have smelled—uh—burning flesh?"

Willie sniffed. "Well—"

But that was as far as he got. The sound of tires crunching on gravel made us all turn around. It was Mrs. McGurk.

2

McGurk Lives!

Can't stop now!" said Mrs. McGurk. "Need to collect a few things. Insurance papers. Dressing gown. Also to dump these . . . oh, dear!"

We stared. The "these" she'd mentioned were a bundle of clothes. McGurk's. I recognized the jeans and the T-shirt. The shirt was spattered with bloodstains. The jeans seemed to have been cut up into at least three pieces.

"Is he all right, Mrs. McGurk?" Wanda called out through the open front door.

"He'll live," came the reply.

"What happened?"

"Later . . ." Mrs. McGurk soon reappeared, carrying a small suitcase. "All I can say is that he's fractured his right leg." She hurried toward the car. "Just how bad"—she tossed the case onto the backseat—"they're finding out right now, before they take him in for surgery."

She switched on the ignition. "Oh, yes!" she groaned, glancing across at the garage. "And would you *please* close those doors? His last request before they took him in for X rays. The *garage doors,* would you believe? He nearly kills himself through not being careful enough changing a dumb lightbulb—common everyday *accident* prevention—and all he can think about is guarding the house against any master criminal who might happen to pass by!"

So we'd been right.

McGurk *had* taken a fall while trying to change the bulb. And during the next few days, while he was in the hospital recovering from the operation, we heard about the other details.

Like number 1: He'd suffered an especially nasty fracture of two bones in his lower right leg. Number 2: But fortunately it wasn't one of those *extra*-especially nasty fractures where the sharp end of a broken bone breaks through the skin. And number 3: The blood had come from a cut in his arm made by a piece of the broken glass.

"And sure," said Mrs. McGurk, the day before he came home, "Dr. Baxter says his leg will make a complete recovery." She frowned. "So long as he keeps off it as much as possible for the first week."

"But when Ed broke *his* leg he was walking about on crutches the day he came home," said Wanda.

"That's because it mustn't have been as complicated," said Mrs. McGurk. "And for goodness' sake don't say anything to *Jack* about that! We'll have trouble enough—keeping him out of that basement, up and down those stairs."

"*We*, ma'am?" I said.

"Yes. I'm counting on you. The reason I've asked you all to keep from visiting him in the hospital is to try not to get him too excited. You know what he's like. He'd hardly come round from the anesthetic before he was babbling about the Organization. How your detective skills would all be getting rusty."

"Oh, boy!" murmured Wanda.

"Exactly!" said Mrs. McGurk. "But don't worry. I think I've found a way around that problem."

Her own hair is much less fiery red than her son's, but there was a gleam in her green eyes that made her look uncannily like him for a second.

"What I've decided on is this—" She paused abruptly, and I could swear she nearly called us "men," just like him. "I've fixed up the guest room on the third floor. Well away from the basement. It has its own private bathroom and refrigerator, so he'll have no excuse for wandering around the rest of the house."

"But—" I began.

"And I've also taken up all the Organization's files and charts and stuff. So that it can be your temporary headquarters while he recovers."

"Sounds great!" said Wanda. "We'll be able to look down on the treetops."

"Yeah!" said Willie. "And we'll be able to stock the refrigerator with snacks and—"

"The refrigerator's only a small one," said Mrs.

McGurk. "Mainly for Jack's orange juice and other soft drinks." She smiled. "But you'll all be free to use the kitchen downstairs to prepare any snacks he—or you—may require."

Which was when I took a long, deep breath. The truth had suddenly hit me.

Just like her son, that lady was all set to *use* us!

I mean, locating him on the third floor instead of his usual second-floor room was a great idea in theory. But in practice it meant she'd have extra stairs to climb when she was attending to the invalid's needs, right?

Wrong!

Because she'd just made sure that the invalid would have five active, energetic, full-time gophers to do all the running around. And with an invalid who was a master at conning others into doing chores and running errands, it looked like we had our work cut out.

When I pointed this out to the others later, their reactions were mixed.

"We'll see about *that!*" said Wanda.

"Though with feeling weak from the operation," said Mari, "perhaps Chief McGurk will be in no condition to give orders."

"No," said Willie. "Maybe the shock's made him a different person. You know—gentle, quiet—uh—timid. Like in that movie where—"

"Hey, yes!" said Brains, our science expert. "It's known as post-traumatic shock syndrome."

I frowned at him—and not only for muscling in on my own territory and using fancy words. "I doubt it," I said.

"Well, I still say he better not try bossing *me* around!" Wanda muttered.

Perhaps Mrs. McGurk had been too optimistic after all. But what none of us had reckoned on—herself included—was the fact that she'd just set the scene for one of the Organization's most puzzling and hazardous investigations yet.

3

The Homecoming

McGurk's homecoming was scheduled for around ten o'clock the following Thursday morning. We were all set to be there, but Mrs. McGurk said no.

"Don't come one minute before eleven."

It turned out she had a problem.

She'd run her great idea in front of him on Wednesday afternoon and he'd objected. They'd been showing a video of an old private eye movie in his ward the evening before. One where business is so bad for the shamus that he can't afford an apartment and has to sleep in his office on an old truckle bed squeezed in between the filing cabinet and the desk.

"No way!" said Mrs. McGurk, when he said that's what he'd prefer: a truckle bed in our basement HQ.

"But, Mom—"

"No *way!*"

Being an invalid, McGurk was even more persistent than usual and kept returning to the argument. In fact, it wasn't until later in the afternoon when Dr. Baxter looked in on the ward that McGurk began to yield. Doc

Baxter happens to be a great Sherlock Holmes fan and McGurk is always ready to listen to *him*.

"*Sherlock* didn't operate out of a beat-up downtown office," he pointed out. "He lived in a luxury apartment, with his colleague Dr. Watson to do the legwork and a housekeeper to look after the cooking and cleaning. That way, his mind was freed up to do all the *real* detective work."

"I think *that* did the trick," said Mrs. McGurk, early on Thursday morning, after putting the finishing touches to the guest room. "Anyway, give me an hour to make sure he's fully adjusted to his new surroundings and we'll expect you back at eleven." She paused. "By the way, you haven't come up with a new case while he's been away, have you?"

We shook our heads, and a flash of disappointment crossed her face.

"Pity!" she muttered. "Any old two-bit case would have done. Just so it grabbed his attention." She looked at us narrowly, beadily. "You *sure*? Not even a missing kitten?"

Again we shook our heads. Then she shrugged. "Oh, well, I guess we can't win 'em all!"

• • •

She must have tried really hard, though.

Because that guy—well, far from grouching about having no case to tackle—greeted us like a Roman emperor just back from an all-conquering campaign.

"Hi, men! Good to see ya! How d'you like our new HQ?"

"It's only temporary!" warned Mrs. McGurk, before she ducked out of the room, leaving us to our reunion.

But McGurk didn't seem to hear her. He was waving his hand airily at the cardboard boxes of files in a neat row on a linen chest and at the neighborhood street map on the opposite wall, pinned to the cork bulletin board from the basement.

For a moment, those file boxes had me worried, wondering if Mrs. McGurk really knew what she was doing, putting them there with their labels shouting out about cases. Labels like this (on several of the boxes):

```
    *       MYSTERIES     *
            ALREADY
            SOLVED
    * * * * * * * * * * * * * * * *
```

And this:

```
    *       LATEST       *
            MYSTERY—

            records &
    *         clues       *
```

Reminding us (and him) every time we glanced that way that we still didn't *have* a latest mystery.

At first, though, we chiefly had eyes for McGurk himself, lying there on a divan, with his back propped up by cushions and pillows, near the big window. It faced south, and the sun was slanting down onto the white plaster encasing his right leg. With the imperial toes just jutting out at the end, it reminded me of the map of Italy. In fact, he *looked* like a Roman emperor just then, especially with a huge bowl of seedless grapes at his elbow.

A rather washed-out Roman emperor, of course. His face was very pale, the freckles around his nose and eyes standing out darkly. But his hair was as fiery as ever and his eyes had a lively enough gleam in them.

"So . . ." he said, popping one of the grapes into his mouth as his eyes rested on me.

Here it comes! I thought. He's going to ask me if we've dug up a new case yet.

"So . . ." he said, moving on.

"I—I like your dressing gown, Chief McGurk," Mari murmured.

It was made of red silk, with green and yellow dragons writhing all over it. It was several sizes too big, having once belonged to his father. But he was wearing it casually flung over his shoulders. Merely for show, I guessed, because it was quite warm in that room.

His eyes had moved on.

"So . . ."

"Terrific view," said Wanda, nodding toward the window. "Perfect for bird watching."

"So . . ."

And then I realized he wasn't thinking about cases at all. He was more interested in what we were holding behind our backs. No longer an emperor. Just an ordinary kid, fresh from the hospital, wondering what get-well *gifts* we'd brought him!

Brains was the first to break.

"Here," he said. "For you, McGurk."

And he thrust forward something long and very thin and not even gift wrapped.

"Aw, you shouldn't have, Officer Bellingham!" said McGurk, not looking terribly thrilled. "What is it?"

"It's an old telescopic car antenna," said our science expert. "Only I've spot-welded it so it doesn't fold up. So it'll reach down inside the plaster to any place where it itches. My father once broke *his* leg and—"

"Just what I wanted!" gasped McGurk, grabbing it. And he set to at once, thrusting it down inside the plaster and scratching away with a look of sheer bliss on his face.

Brains had certainly left the rest of us with one hard act to follow!

But who cares? I was thinking. Just so long as it kept McGurk's mind off the nonexistent new case!

4

McGurk Gets Down to Business

Wanda's offering *might* have topped Brains's. McGurk's expression lit up as he tore the wrapping off the binoculars.

"Aw, you shouldna, Officer Grieg!" he drooled. But his face soon dropped when she said, "That's okay, McGurk. They're my father's but he says he can spare them for a couple of weeks. You know—for watching birds with."

McGurk grunted a word or two of thanks, then turned to Mari.

Her offering was rather bulkier. Bulkier but lighter. He looked most intrigued as he worked on the wrapping. Then his face dropped again.

"A—a *doll*, Officer Yoshimura?"

"One of my glove puppets, Chief McGurk. Those I use in my ventriloquist act. It too is only on loan, but—"

"But I am her very *best* puppet!" the doll suddenly broke in. "So you ought to be really thankful, you big dummy!"

McGurk gaped at the doll and then at Mari.

"Sorry about that, Chief McGurk. But I will give you

some tips on how to throw your *own* voice."

The idea of learning ventriloquism from someone as good at it as our voice expert cheered him up some. He even pulled on the glove and gave it a try.

"Gee, thanks, Officer Yoshimura!" he made the doll say. But there was no mystery about which mouth it was coming from. Especially as he'd just popped another grape into it.

Willie's and my own offerings were outright gifts, bought with our own hard-earned allowance money, and not loans or something we'd found in a junkyard.

Even so...

I mean I can understand Willie's air freshener not exactly making McGurk's day. It was the kind used in cars, in a small plastic container with a suction cup for attaching it to the windshield. "But you can stick it to anything," explained Willie. "The walls, furniture— even—uh—plaster."

"Plaster, Officer Sandowsky?" said McGurk, frowning.

"Ideal for a sickroom," mumbled Willie.

"You said *plaster!*"

Willie gulped. "Yeah, well—you know. Folks with their legs in plaster, they. . ."

"Go *on*, Officer Sandowsky!"

"They don't get a *chance* to wash their feet. I mean, you can't *blame* them. I mean how *can* they?"

I must say *my* nose hadn't noticed anything. Nor had

any of the others', judging by the way they were looking at Willie. But he is the smells expert, after all.

"It's only just in *case*," he said, trying too late to be tactful.

"Huh!" grunted McGurk.

But he did perk up a little as I handed him my gift.

"A book, Officer Rockaway?" he murmured, beginning to pick at the slim, flat package. (I like to make a nice, neat, tight job of my gift wrappings.)

"I bet it's a mystery story, right?" he said, plucking at the tape. "Or a book of *mini*-mysteries—which I'll solve in record time—but it's a kind thought," he said, when he'd finally worked his way down to the colored paper. "And at least it'll keep me from getting rusty and—*aw*!"

This time it wasn't *aw*! as in "aw, you shouldna!" This was an *aw*! of downright disappointment.

"A notebook! Just like the ones *you* use!"

"Sure," I said. "But it's brand new and the best quality. I thought you could use it while you're stuck in bed. For jotting down any thoughts on crime and detection that—"

"But, Officer Rockaway," he said, "why would I need a notebook when I've got all *this* to jot my notes on?"

He was gently tapping the plaster. The stretch that ran from the knee to the top edge. All smooth and white and (so far) unblemished.

"This space," he said, "is reserved for me. You guys

may now sign your autographs anywhere below the
knee . . . oh, and help yourselves to a grape while you're
doing it," he added, grandly waving at the now nearly
empty bowl.

"I thought you'd never ask, McGurk," said Wanda.

• • •

Now that plaster cast and the notes on it were soon going to figure very importantly in our investigations. So
let me just present you with this:

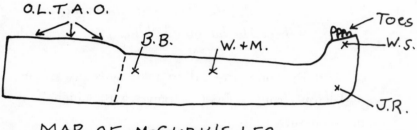

MAP OF McGURK'S LEG

O.L.T.A.O. means that this space was Off-Limits To
All Officers, and strictly reserved for McGurk himself.

B.B. is where Brains Bellingham left *his* get-well
message (and a very messy one it was, too!).

W. & M. stands for where Wanda and Mari parked
their joint effort.

J.R. is where I made my contribution.

And W.S.—that's where Willie left *his* scrawl.

The actual messages, in order of being inscribed,
were:

#1 Roses are red, violets are blue,
   Brambles are prickly and so are you!
      Wanda Grieg. Mari Yoshimura.

#2 By hook or by crook, I'll be the last on this foot!
      W. Sandowsky.

That one gave me the idea for where to locate mine.

#3 This won't last forever, It isn't for real,
   So cheer up, McGurk. Your leg will soon heal!
      Signed: J. Rockaway (on the heel of a
      heel. Ha, ha! only kidding!)

#4 And this one seemed to take ages, as Brains copied it out from a sheet of paper with which he'd come ready prepared.

"What kind of language is *that*?" asked McGurk. "Chinese?"

"I don't think so," murmured Mari. "Bird tracks in the snow, perhaps?"

"Fencing positions?" I suggested.

"Little men waving?" said Willie.

"Close, Willie," said Brains. "Actually, it's semaphore. Usually the little guys carry flags. But I thought it might take too long, so I've just shown the position of their arms."

"What's it say?" McGurk asked suspiciously.

"Something some guy wrote on my *dad's* plaster," said Brains. "Only in ordinary English."

"*What*, Officer Bellingham? Wrote *what*?"

"Uh—well—" said Brains, "taking it line by line— uh—*Some...guys...get all...the...breaks.*" He looked anxiously at McGurk. "A—uh—joke. Kind of. That last line is my initials—*G.B. G* for Gerald, *B* for—"

"I know, I know!" McGurk sounded irritable. But his face soon brightened. "Not bad, Officer Bellingham! The code, I mean."

Then, vastly relieved, Brains brightened too. "Yes, I thought you'd like it, McGurk! And look—I've brought a photocopy of the full semaphore alphabet. So you can learn it. It might come in handy one day."

"Hm!" I murmured, while Brains babbled on. I bent a little closer, wondering if anyone else had spotted the glaring error. I reached for the photocopied alphabet.

"Like when we're out on a case somewhere," Brains concluded, "and we need to send messages over a distance. When we don't have any two-way radios."

"I like it, I like it!" said McGurk. "Officer Rockaway, you're the word expert. Why don't *you* learn it too?"

"Yes, Joey," said Brains, smirking. "Why don't you?"

"That's just what I'm doing." I pointed to the last character. "If this is *B* for Bellingham, and this last word of the message is *breaks*, how come it, too, doesn't start with a *B*?"

"Huh?" grunted Brains. "But it—well—it—it—"

"If the rest of the message is correct," I said, "the way it reads is: 'Some guys get all the *freaks*.' You put an *F* instead of a *B*."

"Is that so, Officer Bellingham?" McGurk growled.

"Oh—uh—yeah. . ." Blushing to the roots of his short, bristly, fair hair, Brains was rapidly looking from the photocopied alphabet to McGurk's leg and back again.

"Well, get it corrected!" said McGurk. "A mistake like that could cost an officer's *life* out in the field!"

Then, when Brains was through, McGurk folded his arms, sat up very straight, and said, "Right!"

Just that one word—but it was enough to make my heart sink.

With the newly decorated leg stretched out in front of him, the various gifts and loans strewn on the divan at either side, and the grape bowl now empty, he suddenly looked very beady-eyed and businesslike.

"Party's over, men! It's time for your reports on all the possible new cases you've been looking into during my absence."

5

Mutiny?

So the moment of reckoning had come. And we had nothing to say.

Curiously enough, he didn't hit the roof. I guessed he'd already found out the truth. All he did was shake his head sadly.

"And there was I, thinking I'd have to choose which case out of the four or five you'd all have come up with. Which case would be the most challenging." He ended with a heavy sigh. "Oh, well! It can't be helped, I guess."

"Darned right it can't!" said Wanda. "We were all too worried about *you* to go grubbing around looking for cases."

"You bet!" said Willie. "And your accident *was* a case at first. A real mystery."

"The basement in darkness," said Mari.

"The house deserted," said Wanda.

"The overturned chairs, the broken glass," I said.

"The blood," said Brains.

"We didn't know *what* could have happened to you," said Wanda.

"A real mystery," Willie said again. "And we solved *that*!"

McGurk had listened with a strange expression—kind of wistful. Then I realized what it was when he sighed again and said: "It took you long enough!"

The guy was regretting he hadn't been there to investigate his own disappearance!

"Anyway, McGurk," said Wanda, "you're in no condition to go running around—uh—*hopping* around on crutches—solving mysteries!"

"Oh, *I* wouldn't have had to do any running around," he replied. "Which reminds me. Mom says you guys will be helping to look after me. Well, it looks like you've cleaned me out of grapes. I think there's still some downstairs, but if not, just ask Mom and she'll give you the money to get some more. And if you'll just see how I'm fixed for tortilla chips. . . ."

Well, okay. We'd come prepared to help out, and it was a big relief after expecting him to go on and on and on, beefing about having no case.

But we hadn't reckoned on his deep cunning. . . .

At first it was just straight errands, like the grapes and the chips. Sometimes it was in-house errands, like going down to the kitchen or to the basement. Sometimes it was around-the-premises errands, like to the garage or the backyard. And sometimes it was an away-from-house errand, like to the supermarket or to the candy store when McGurk suddenly had a yearning for peanut brittle.

And at first we didn't really mind. After all, Mrs.

McGurk was paying and we were helping him eat those grapes and chips and peanut brittle and stuff. But by midafternoon we were beginning to tire. And that's when he struck.

"How many times have you been down to the kitchen today?" he asked mildly, as we all lay flopped around on various chairs and cushions.

"Five," I said.

"At least," sighed Brains.

"Some of us more," grunted Wanda.

"Yes," said Mari, patiently.

"I make it nine," said Willie. "But that's because I forgot what I'd went for a few times, and had to do it again."

"Whatever," said McGurk. "So here's a test of your observation powers. How many oranges in those hanging fruit baskets?"

"Oh, lots," said Wanda. "Who's had time to count?"

"You shouldn't need time," said McGurk. "A good detective would have registered them automatically."

"Ten!" said Brains.

"At least a dozen," I said.

"Some of them were tangerines," said Willie. "I smelled tangerines. *I'd* guess four tangerines and eight oranges."

"Okay," murmured McGurk, looking up from the plaster cast, where he'd been jotting down our estimates. "Officer Yoshimura?"

"Oh—uh—seven, Chief McGurk."

"Officer Grieg—you still want to leave it at *lots*?"

"Go on, then," said Wanda. "I'll go with seven, like Mari."

"Right," said McGurk. "So why don't you all go down now and check . . . oh, and just stick four of them onto the juicer. You ought to know by now I like my juice fresh. Hey, and don't forget to remove the pith!"

The correct answer was thirteen oranges and three tangerines, much to our embarrassment. And from then on we couldn't go anywhere without having to face an observation test on our return.

Like:

> What is the make of the blender?
>
> What color or colors are the tiles on the kitchen floor?

Or (moving out of the house):

> How many pickets missing from the south side fence?
>
> How many plant pots in the stack in the garage?

Then, away from the McGurk house:

> What is the registration number of Dave Braff's gray Chevy parked outside the Braff house across the road?

(The jerk could see this through the binoculars as he lay there sipping his cool, fresh, pith-free orange juice. Whereas we of course hadn't even given it a thought as we hurried past under the hot sun, our heads filled with his latest shopping list!

"Anyway," Wanda had said, "we *know* it's Dave's. We *know* he always parks it there when he gets home late after hanging out with my brother Ed and some of the other seniors. We *know* he parks it there so that the driveway is clear in the morning when his father sets out for work. So why *would* we want to memorize the number?" "To train your powers of observation," was McGurk's answer to that. "And to keep them razor sharp at all times.")

There were also the even trickier car questions, like:

How many cars were in the disabled driver spaces at the shopping plaza?

(a) when we arrived?

(b) when we left?

(c) Did all the cars occupying those spaces carry genuine disabled driver stickers?

(d) If not, what were their makes, models, colors, and numbers?

• • •

Come Friday morning, I for one was taking no chances. I must have filled at least ten pages of my notebook with details of various store clerks' estimated heights, weights, and eye colors—not to mention page after page of car numbers.

Here's an example:

Supermarket checkout Lady
on the Less-than-10-Items line.

Name (on tag): DOLLY

Hair color: Black
Eye color: Brown
Estimated height: 5 ft. 3 in. (slightly
                        taller than Wanda)
Est. weight: 110 lbs
Distinguishing marks, etc.: Green cross on
              gold chain around neck.
Close-bitten fingernails.
Rather nervous about people
        staring at her.
Very nervous about people
    staring at her and
    writing in notebooks.

And let me admit right now that McGurk's question on that occasion wasn't even *about* the checkout lady. It was about (a) the customer in front of us, and (b) the customer just behind us.

It did put us all on our toes, though, boosting our powers of observation at least one thousand percent. But at the same time we were so exhausted that *physically* we were right down flat on our heels with sagging knees.

And toward the end of Friday afternoon, there was something in the air even stronger than the rich aroma of the toasted cheese sandwich McGurk had had for lunch and the Mountain Pines odor of Willie's freshener.

And the name of that something?

Mutiny! What else? Blazing, boiling, bubbling mutiny!

6

"Something very weird!"
–A Question of Gender

We still felt sore the following morning, and we all agreed when Wanda phoned around suggesting we meet up at the corner of Sycamore and Elm before going to see McGurk.

"This can't go on!" she said, as soon as we were assembled there at nine. "There's a whole week yet before we go back to school!"

Our faces fell even further. Normally, the idea of going back to school is a matter of slight sadness if not downright grief. But now it couldn't come soon *enough*.

"I'm counting the days," said Brains.

"Yeah," said Willie. "Me, too! Eight more to go."

"Nine, counting today," said Mari.

"He'll have run us ragged long before then," I said.

"He's just using us as *slaves*!" said Wanda. "It's sheer exploitation. Especially for us girls. And if he addresses us as 'men' just one more time. . ."

We'd been drifting along toward the McGurk house. Wanda didn't get to finish because just then we were interrupted by angry voices across the road. It was Mr. Braff and Dave. Dave's car was in the driveway. So was Mr. Braff, glaring up at a bedroom window and yelling to Dave to get down and move his car immediately. By this time we'd reached the McGurk driveway. Mrs. McGurk was standing at the front door.

"Thank goodness you're here!" she said. "He's been getting very impatient."

"I'll *bet* he has!" muttered Wanda.

"Please hurry!" urged Mrs. McGurk. "I've never seen him in such a state."

"Is it his leg, Mrs. McGurk?" I asked, suddenly anxious.

"No. He said it was an Organization thing." She ushered us in to the foot of the stairs and motioned us to go ahead. "More than that, he wouldn't say."

"Probably he's fresh out of peanut brittle," said Wanda, when we reached the second floor. Then she looked up. "Is that him now, thumping on the floor? Just wait until—"

Then she stopped at the open doorway to McGurk's room.

Yes, he *had* been thumping the floor with one of his crutches. But as he turned from the window his voice wasn't at all loud with impatience. His first words, half croaked, were: "Freeze! All of you! Approach the window with caution!"

He looked grave. Also very perplexed.

"Why?" I whispered. "What's wrong, McGurk?"

"I—" he cast an uneasy glance at the window. "I've just seen something very weird!"

"*What*?" It was Wanda who sounded impatient now.

I wondered if it had something to do with Mr. Braff and Dave's car and the ruckus across the road. But I was wrong.

McGurk glanced at the stretch of plaster above his knee, where he'd scribbled some notes.

"I've just seen a frail, white-haired old lady scratching her head. In a wheelchair. Down in the Mayroyd backyard."

"So what?" said Wanda. "What's weird about an old woman scratching her head?"

"She took off her hair first, that's what. It was a wig. And under it—*she was bald!*"

That pulled us up!

Then Brains said, "Well—maybe she's sick. Maybe—"

"Not completely *hairless*," said McGurk. "Just regular bald. On top. With dark hair around the back and above the ears. That frail old lady is a *guy*. Midforties is my estimate. And I bet she—*he*—isn't all that frail, either!"

Well. . . We looked at one another. Was this just another of McGurk's ruses to bring us to heel? Had he sensed our rebellious mood?

He glanced out again. "He's gone indoors now. But there's something fishy going on down there, men. We might have a case on our hands."

The suspicious glint in Wanda's eyes had been gradually fading, but now it returned in a flash.

"Just one thing, McGurk," she said.

"What?"

"You just called us 'men.'"

"So what if I did?"

"Two of us are females," said Wanda.

"Come on, Officer Grieg! What is this? You know darned well that when I say 'men' I mean 'officers.'"

"Why don't you call us officers, then?"

He rolled his eyes.

"I do call you officers, Officer Grieg!"

"She means collectively, McGurk," I said. "Like anyone else might say 'guys' or 'folks.'"

"Guys or folks are *civilians*, Officer Rockaway!"

Which is when Willie stepped in with the clincher. (That kid is full of surprises.)

"Lieutenant Carmichael calls *his* officers—men and women both—he calls them 'people.' Like, 'Come on, people, let's get with it!'"

McGurk's jaw sagged. Then his eyes lit up. Willie had just hit him where he lived. Lieutenant Carmichael of the NYPD is McGurk's favorite TV hero. Wasn't the lieutenant another fresh orange juice freak?

"Oh—uh—yes. You're right, Officer Sandowsky." He clapped his hands. "Okay, people, let's get with it. Like I said—something fishy's going on down there."

"Yes," I murmured, suddenly stiffening. "And I think she—he's—just come out again!"

The others rushed past me to catch a glimpse of the white-haired figure slowly gliding across the Mayroyd patio in a wheelchair.

"Back!" growled McGurk, lifting the binoculars. "Not so close!"

"She won't see us from there," said Brains. "We're behind glass. All she'll see is the sun's reflection."

"And he isn't even looking this way," said Mari.

Note that. Brains said "she." Mari said "he." I guess we still weren't one hundred percent sure whether McGurk had been putting us on or not.

Then something happened that left us in no doubt.

The wheelchair person had moved behind some rose-bushes but was now emerging again. And sure enough—shoulder-length white hair, long flowery dress. What else *could* she be but a poor disabled old lady?

"McGurk," I began, "if that's a guy, then I'm a blue-tailed—"

But that's when we saw the invalid reach up and begin scratching his head.

Oh, yes! *His*, all right!

And oh, no! This time he didn't take off the wig first.

It was more horrible than that.

He simply slid his hand under it, slowly, seemingly absentmindedly, until first his fingers disappeared, then the rest of his hand, and the wig started to jiggle up and down like there was a live rat or a ferret trapped there.

7

Disguise?

It was only for a few seconds. Suddenly, the hand was withdrawn and the wheelchair person looked toward the house's open sliding door. Then he nodded, glanced this way and that, patted the wig, and went back inside the house.

"I think someone called her—him—in," said Willie.

"Yeah," said McGurk. "There's a man and a woman in there. I tell you, there's something very strange going on, men—uh—people."

"But that doesn't make it a *case*, McGurk," I said. "Even if the one in the wheelchair *is* a man—maybe he just feels more comfortable dressed like that."

"More comfortable?" said McGurk. "With that wig bugging him? He just isn't used to wearing it. Anyone can see that."

"So?" I said.

"So it's obviously temporary," said McGurk. "A disguise. And disguises mean something crooked's going down. And that makes it a case. Okay?"

"But what *kind* of case, McGurk?" Brains asked.

"Why would he need to disguise himself?"

"That's what we have to find out," said McGurk, giving his leg a thoughtful stirring with Brains's antenna—something he'd been doing ever since he'd seen the man scratching away under the wig. "Maybe he's on the FBI's Ten Most Wanted list."

"Yes," said Wanda. "Or maybe it's to make the neighbors think it's just a harmless little bunch of people come to live here."

"Hey, yeah!" said Willie. "While they're really planning to pull off a big-time crime!"

"Not so fast, Willie," I said. "How long *have* they been living there, McGurk? *I've* never seen the wheelchair person before."

"That's because they only got here last night," said McGurk. "Him and a middle-aged couple. I saw them arrive, just before seven. I figured it was another bunch of tenants renting the Mayroyd place for a month or two."

We nodded. Professor Mayroyd and his family were over in Europe for a three-year spell and they'd decided to rent out their house, furnished. Usually the tenants were folks who needed someplace to stay while they looked around for permanent homes of their own. Rather dull, respectable people as a rule. The only reason we were ever interested in them was to judge their attitude toward the vacant lot between the McGurk house and theirs—a glorious jungle of weeds and bushes. McGurk liked to use it for training sessions. It too belonged to the Mayroyds but none of the tenants ever seemed to be aware of the fact.

McGurk was gazing down at that vacant lot right now.

"The weeds are pretty thick over by the Mayroyd fence," he murmured.

I stirred uneasily. It was one of his father's regular beefs—how those weeds threatened to invade the McGurk yard. Sometimes he'd order McGurk to chop them down before their seeds blew over. Which meant training sessions for us. *How to Search Overgrown Terrain for Vital Clues* was his favorite.

"Yes," murmured Wanda, with a thoughtful gleam in *her* eyes, too, "and that old crabapple tree would make a very convenient observation post."

McGurk nodded. "Good thinking, Officer Grieg. . . ."

Which is a convenient point to present this copy of the map I made of that corner of the neighborhood:

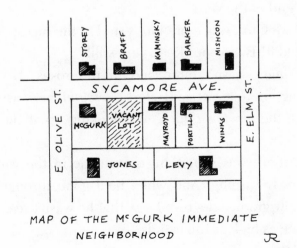

MAP OF THE McGURK IMMEDIATE
NEIGHBORHOOD

"If you're thinking what I'm thinking," Wanda said, "why don't we—"

"Here's the couple now!" McGurk cut in.

The man and woman stepped out onto the patio. The man was tall and thin. He was wearing a light tan suit and a button-down collar and necktie despite the heat. The woman was also neatly dressed, but far more suitably, with a blue halter top and Bermuda shorts.

"Take a good look, people," said McGurk, handing the binoculars to Wanda. "I want you to be able to recognize them instantly, next time you see them."

Wanda was already busy focusing. "Now that *is* a woman," she murmured. "A man might pass himself off as a woman, sitting down. But she—you can tell by the way she walks."

The woman was strolling in front of the rosebushes, bending to sniff at them from time to time, on her way to the end of the yard.

But McGurk was more interested in the man.

"Hold it! Everyone! Keep very still!"

The *man* wasn't interested in the roses. He was standing there erect and alert. *Possibly* he was only sniffing the air. *Possibly* he was looking up at the few clouds.

But there was something systematic in the way he was slowly turning. And when he'd gone through another few gradual degrees I saw that he wasn't scanning anything as high as the clouds.

That guy was inspecting the neighboring houses! Casually, maybe. Purely interested in the kind of neighborhood he'd come to live in, perhaps.

But as I said: very systematically, suddenly reminding me of a presidential bodyguard, alert for snipers. When he paused, facing the direction of the Jones house, I became aware of the sound of Mr. Jones's power mower.

"I think he's checking"—I began—"to see if anyone"—the man's head slowly resumed its rotation—"might have spotted the wheelchair person—fooling around—with the wig. . . ."

My voice had dropped to a dry whisper.

"You sure about him not being able to see *us*, Officer Bellingham?" said McGurk.

"I—I think so. . ." said Brains. It had been his turn to use the binoculars and he'd lowered them rapidly.

But the systematic gaze continued on past the McGurk house without any noticeable pause, and we began to breathe more easily.

"He doesn't *look* like a crook," said Brains.

"He looks like he might be a college professor himself," said Wanda. "A colleague of Mr. Mayroyd's, perhaps."

"*She* doesn't look like a crook either," I said, as the couple went back inside the house.

"Maybe they are just house hunting after all," said Mari. "With an eccentric son or brother who thinks he is a woman."

"Yeah!" gasped Willie. "Like that guy in the movie who went around stabbing folks while they were taking a shower! *He* thought he was his own mother and—"

"You're jumping the gun, Officer Sandowsky!" snapped McGurk. "Guessing. There *may* be a simple explanation. But as good detectives we have to find out *for sure* what's going on. And here's how I want you all to proceed. . . ."

8

Three Assignments

F irst thing we do is double-check that the wheelchair person really is a guy," said McGurk.

"But you said you'd seen his bald head!" Brains protested.

"Yes, Officer Bellingham, and *you* said it might be an old lady who'd lost her hair through illness."

"Sure. But then *you* said you'd seen the dark hair that was left."

"I *know!*" McGurk was scowling. "But I was taken by surprise, remember."

"So now you're doubting what you've seen, McGurk," said Wanda. "Your lightning powers of observation just weren't up to snuff."

"Of course they were!" he snapped. "It's just that— well—it could have been a trick of the light." He glared around at us. "It's just that it wouldn't stand up as evidence in *court!*"

"So you think we should double-check?" I said. "How?"

"We use *another* of our senses, Officer Rockaway."

"Our noses?" said Willie, brightening.

"No. Our *ears*. We check the sound of the person's

voice. If it's a man's or a woman's."

"From *here,* Chief McGurk?" said Mari, glancing down at the Mayroyd house.

"No, Officer Yoshimura. From down there. Which is where *you* come in."

"You mean you want Mari to eavesdrop on their conversation?" said Wanda. "What about their rights? Aren't you forgetting people are supposed to be innocent until—"

"I know all that!" said McGurk. "I'm only asking Officer Yoshimura to check on the *sound* of that person's voice. Even if no one else is out there. Just a cough would be enough. Just a clearing of the throat. Right, Officer Yoshimura?"

"Yes, Chief McGurk. A cough, certainly. . ."

"Or if he or she gets stung by a bee and hollers out?"

"No problem, Chief McGurk."

McGurk's eyes were gleaming. "So that's your assignment, Officer Yoshimura. I want you to go down into the lot with officers Grieg and Bellingham as cover."

"Cover?" said Wanda.

"Yes. Just three kids fooling around. Looking for a lost ball, playing hide and seek, picking wildflowers. Anything, so long as you're close enough to hear him cough or sneeze."

"But he isn't out there," said Wanda.

"No, but he may come out again at any time," said McGurk.

"What about *us*?" I asked. "Willie and me?"

"For you, Officers Rockaway and Sandowsky, I have special duties. Yours, Officer Sandowsky, is to go along Sycamore, past the Mayroyd house, and check on the car."

"Car?" said Willie, looking out.

"Probably parked in the driveway," said McGurk. "If it is, check its make, model, and color. I only caught a glimpse of it yesterday. Some kind of station wagon, I think. Oh, and take its number, too. And any other distinguishing marks."

Willie was looking overwhelmed. "But what if it's in the garage?"

"Well, let's just hope they left the door open," said McGurk. "Most people do when their car's inside during the day."

"But I can't just walk in there and *study* the car!"

"Darned right you can't, Officer Sandowsky! You do this casually, in passing. Even if it takes you a dozen times around the block to get the details one at a time."

"But what if I forget? If there are so many—"

"Here. Take this," said McGurk, handing Willie the notebook I'd given him. "But don't let them see you writing in it. Wait until you've gotten past the Mayroyd house."

Well! I was speechless! My get-well gift! The jerk was handing that brand-new top-quality notebook to a schmuck who'd be sure to cover the pages with blots, smudges, crossings-out, and who knows what else!

"Shouldn't *I* be doing that, McGurk?" I asked.

"No. You've got a trickier task, Officer Rockaway. An interview."

That took some of the sting out. "An interview with the people down *there*? At the Mayroyd—"

"No. Right now I want you to ask Mr. Jones if *he* knows anything about them."

"If *he* doesn't, nobody will," said Wanda. "A regular old gossip like him."

"But what will I say?" I objected. "I can't just tell him we suspect they're a bunch of crooks."

McGurk sighed. "What you say, Officer Rockaway, is this. That you've come with a message from me. Thanking him and Mrs. Jones for their get-well card. And then, kind of casually, you say, 'Oh, by the way, Jack's noticed we have some new neighbors.'"

"That's all?"

"You bet," he replied. "With a guy like him that'll be enough." He turned to the others. "Okay, people! Let's get with it!"

"One thing, McGurk," said Brains.

"Yes, Officer Bellingham?"

"Could I just take five minutes to rush home—"

"For *what*, Officer Bellingham?"

"To get my photocopy of the semaphore code. So when we're down there, if the person comes out and coughs or gets bitten or stung..."

"Go on." McGurk was sounding interested.

"And Mari identifies the voice, I'll be able to signal the result up to you. Instantly. *M* or *F*. Male or Female."

"Good thinking, Officer Bellingham!" McGurk looked pleased. Then he frowned. "But I have a photocopy of the code already. Here, see."

"Yes, but I don't," said Brains. "Not with me. And I haven't gotten around to memorizing it yet."

"Oh, for Pete's sake!" exclaimed Wanda. "Memorize it *now*, then! Just those two letters, *M* and *F*."

"No," said McGurk. "Go ahead, Officer Bellingham. You may need to add something vital and urgent. Which I can then jot down on my leg."

"Oh, boy!" muttered Wanda.

I knew what she was thinking. This: Trust McGurk to get hooked on a fancy idea like that! When all it needed was to forget about semaphoring anyway, and just use something simple. Like Brains scratching his head for female or rubbing his chin for male.

But who was I to make things easier for a jerk who'd spurned my gift the way McGurk had?

"Come on, Willie," I said. "*We* don't need semaphore signals and plaster casts. We have our good old-fashioned, totally reliable, foolproof notebooks!"

9

Mixed Signals

McGurk had been right, though, when he said all I'd have to do was simply mention the new neighbors.

"Oh, sure," said Mr. Jones, settling himself more comfortably on the seat of his mower. "They seem a nice couple. Name of Robinson. He's just taken early retirement. Some kind of high-up bank executive out in California. Thinking of settling in these parts. They're house hunting. With Mr. Robinson's old mother. An invalid lady."

As he spoke, Mr. Jones waved at a cloud of gnats around his head as if it were a cloud of information from which he was plucking these details. A kind of computer data bank.

I was impressed. Those people had arrived less than twenty-four hours ago!

"Have you met them already?" I asked.

"Well, not exactly," he said. "I just heard about them. From Myra Wilenchick. She works at W. B. Realtors, you know. The agents dealing with the Mayroyd rental.

I saw her last week, when she came to check the property. . . But I tell a lie! I did *sort* of meet the old lady. About an hour ago."

"The one in the wheelchair?"

"Yes. When I was emptying the grass box onto the compost heap. I caught a glimpse of her white hair the other side of the lilac bushes. She'd been looking back up toward Sycamore and across the vacant lot. Mr. Braff was having a run-in with Dave. He was yelling up at Dave, who was at his bedroom window. Their voices were carrying clear across the vacant lot and you could hear every word. Seems the kid had parked his Chevy in the driveway, blocking Mr. Braff's exit. Dave said he didn't think it mattered, being Saturday morning, and Mr. Braff said that Dave ought to know by now that there were some Saturdays—yeah, and Sundays, too— when he, Mr. Braff, had to put in extra time at the office. It was part of the responsibility of being in command, he said. 'Not that *you'd* know about *that*!' he went on. 'Lying in bed until—' "

"Yes, sir," I said, cutting in. "But you were telling me about the old lady."

"Oh, yes. . . Well, I said, 'Hi, nice morning, ma'am!' But she just dipped her head and went wheeling away back up the path. Shy, maybe. Some old folks get like that, especially when they're invalids. How's *your* invalid, by the way?"

I made my notes on my way back. Here's a copy:

Interview with Mr. Jones, re:
new neighbors

Name of newcomers: ROBINSON
(Mr. & Mrs. & Mr. R's mother)

Details: Recently retired bank
executive from California.
Househunting. (According
to Mr. J's informant: Ms. M.
Wilenchick of W. B. Realtors.)

MOST IMPORTANT!
Mr. J's encounter with Mrs. R.
(Senior) at end of yard. Refused
to return his greeting. Dipped
head & wheeled back to house.
Mr. Jones thinks she must be
shy.

I, J.R., think it confirms our
suspicions!!! ***

I was very proud of those notes as I hurried up the
stairs.

"Hey, McGurk!" I said. "Wait till you see—"

He waved me quiet. He was peering through the
binoculars.

"Where are the others?" I said.

"Down there," he grunted.

"I don't see anyone."

The vacant lot seemed deserted. I couldn't see any-one out on Sycamore. There was no one visible in the McGurk yard, or even on the Mayroyd patio.

"You're not *supposed* to," murmured McGurk. "They're playing hide and seek. Down in the lot. I've lost 'em myself."

"Well, which one is *seeking*?"

"It doesn't matter. Just so long as Officer Yoshimura is in position for when the subject comes out again."

I brightened. "Hey, talking of the wheelchair guy, you'll never guess what Mr. Jones had to say. About meeting him this morning."

"Huh?" McGurk nearly dropped the binoculars as he swung around. "Why didn't you tell me this imme-diately?"

"Read my notes," I said.

"Nice work, Officer Rockaway!" he kept muttering, as he pored over them. And: "Yeah, that would figure!" And: "Shy, my foot!"

It was a pleasure to see the effect they had on him as he went over them again and again, with his eyes gleaming brighter and brighter. The others would have to get very lucky to top *that*, I was thinking, as I glanced down at the still deserted-seeming vacant lot.

And here's a good point at which to insert the more detailed plan I made later:

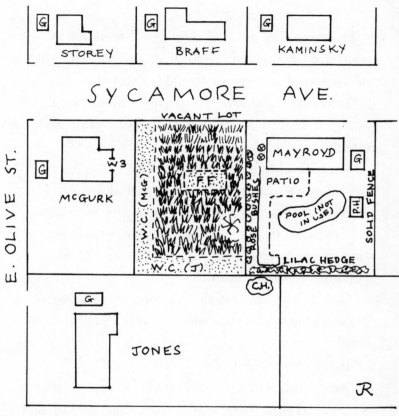

KEY G = Garages
W3 = McGurk's 3rd floor window
FF = Foundations of abandoned guest cottage
W.C. = Spaces kept cleared by Mr. Jones and Mr. McGurk
for weed control
✳ = Crabapple tree
⊗ = Mayroyd garbage cans
P.H. = Pool house
C.H. = Compost heap (Jones yard)

"Are you *sure* the others are down there, McGurk?" I said, after a while.

He looked up from my notes.

"They better be!" He lifted the binoculars. "Yeah. . . Officer Grieg's still in the crab tree. I can just see the sole of one of her feet, near the top. She must be lying full-length on one of the branches. . ."

He slowly shifted the angle of the binoculars.

"Officer Yoshimura *should* be somewhere in the weeds near the Mayroyd fence. . . ."

This was where the weeds were three or four feet high.

"Yes," said McGurk. "I just saw those black-eyed Susans move. A few feet in front of the tree. Near the corner of those old foundations."

There was no telltale movement in the black-eyed Susans when *I* looked.

"What about Brains?"

McGurk shrugged. "Somewhere in the long grass this side of the tree. . . I think."

"How long are they supposed to stay there?" I asked. "I mean, there's no sign of anyone coming out onto the patio again."

"That sliding door's still open," said McGurk. "So those three officers remain on task."

He sounded very determined.

"Here's Willie, anyway," I said, turning.

Our smells expert looked very pleased with himself.

"The details!" he said, holding out the notebook. "It took me seven times around the block, but I got 'em!"

"What's all *this*?" growled McGurk, wrinkling his nose.

Just as I'd feared, the first few pages of that lovely new notebook looked like a disaster area.

"The details!" Willie repeated. "See?"—he pointed to a mass of tangled lines with words shooting off in every direction—"*Brown Olds Station Wagon*."

"You mean that's what it says?" grumbled McGurk. "Somewhere in all this garbage?"

"Well, it isn't *easy*, trying to write standing up," said Willie. "Sometimes on the move. Is it, Joey?"

"Don't ask me," I murmured.

"And this?" said McGurk, stabbing a finger at the second page. "Are these *numbers*?"

"Sure," said Willie. "The car's. It took me four tries to get them right. They kept slipping outa my mind. But *those* are good. At the end there."

"So what's this about *Any Place*?"

"Give me that!" said Willie. He peered, then grinned. "No, McGurk! That first *A* is where I bumped into a tree while I was writing it down. That says *N.Y. Plates*. The license plates. New York."

"Okay," sighed McGurk, turning to the third page. "And I suppose this, *these*, are notes about the car, too?"

"Yes," said Willie, looking hurt. "Can't you *read*, McGurk? What it says is—" He peered closer. "Oh, yes—'Officer unable to get close enough, but car in very'—I think that's 'messy' but it could be 'muddy'—'and dirty condition.'"

McGurk looked all set to give Willie a piece of his mind about the condition of those notes when I spotted a sudden movement down below.

"Brains," I said. "I think he's got something."

Our science expert had just reared up from the long grass, staring up at McGurk's window. In one hand he had the semaphore code photocopy. In the other, he was flapping a yellow silk handkerchief. I guessed he was going to signal us, using them as flags. But first he seemed to be studying the code more closely.

"Oh, come on, Officer Bellingham!" groaned McGurk. "*M* or *F*?"

"I don't think Mari could have heard the wheelchair guy cough or sneeze inside the house," I said. "It looks like this might be something more vital and urgent."

"You really think so, Officer Rockaway? Uh—here..." McGurk passed me his own photocopy. "You take this and jot his message down in your notebook.... When he gets around to it!"

"You sure you wouldn't like *Willie* to jot it down in your notebook?"

"Get with it, Officer Rockaway! He's starting!"

For the next few minutes, as Brains flapped and fumbled and fluttered, I had my work cut out. Fortunately, he was having to signal as slowly as I was having to interpret the letters, and toward the end I was getting quicker at it.

Meanwhile, Wanda had climbed down from the tree and Mari had emerged from the weeds. Both were looking over Brains's shoulders. There was still no sign of anyone in the Mayroyd yard.

"Well? That it?" said McGurk, when Brains finally mopped his forehead with the yellow "flag."

"Seems like it," I said. I passed him what I had written down—this:

"*Walta?*" McGurk said.

"Possibly *Walter*. That must be Mr. Robinson's name. Or the wheelchair person's."

"Hey, yeah!" said McGurk, suddenly oozing confidence again. "A vital clue. If Officer Yoshimura heard a man's voice in there calling out '*Walter*' to another person, that has to mean the wheelchair person."

"So what's this *nows?*" said Willie. "We know he has a nose."

"Wait a minute!" I said. "Could be a mistake in transmission. Maybe that's *Wanda,* not *Walta.*"

McGurk scowled. "Yeah! And maybe that's *news* not *nows.* 'Wanda has news.'"

"Well, don't look at me!" I said. "That's what he signaled."

"Whatever!" growled McGurk. "But what kind of news?"

"We'll soon know," said Willie.

Sure enough, we could hear rapid footsteps coming up the stairs. Then: "You're not going to believe this, McGurk!" Wanda sang out, as they all burst into the room.

"Believe what, Officer Grieg?"

"From where I was I could see partway inside their dining room."

"So?"

"So I saw something very interesting indeed."

"What? Come *on*, Officer Grieg!"

Everyone was staring at her, including Mari and Brains. She'd obviously been keeping it to herself.

"I saw," said Wanda, calmly, taking her time, "I saw the man with the suit. Only in there he'd taken off his jacket."

"And you call that interesting, Officer Grieg?"

"You bet I do, McGurk. Because—are you ready for this?"

"Get on with your report, Officer Grieg! Ready for *what*?"

"The fact that the tall man carries a gun. In a shoulder holster. I saw it quite clearly."

10

~

FBI Agents?

McGurk had been scratching his leg. But now he stopped abruptly. "Are you sure it was a gun, Officer Grieg?"

"Positive!"

McGurk's eyes remained narrowed. "Did you see it?"

"Well. . . the shoulder holster. . . sure."

McGurk resumed his prodding with the antenna. "Could you see the gun itself? Like maybe the butt?"

"Well, from where I was—not *exactly*. But, I mean, a shoulder holster, like police detectives wear on TV—what else could it be?"

The mention of police detectives seemed to ring a bell. The prodding scratching became more rhythmical, as McGurk asked me to refill his glass with orange juice.

"Could it a been a tool holder?" said Willie. "Like handymen wear?"

Wanda gave Willie a scornful look. "No one carries wrenches and screwdrivers and stuff around in a *shoulder* holster!"

"Maybe it's for some scientific instrument," Brains

said. "A calculator, maybe. Maybe he's an architect or a surveyor or a—"

"Be quiet, Officer Bellingham!" McGurk put down his empty glass with a slam. "Officer Grieg says it was like detectives wear on TV and she's right. Lieutenant Carmichael has one. All his officers wear them. Go on, Officer Grieg. You say this guy had taken his coat off?"

"Sure. How else would I have seen the holster? And that was another interesting thing."

"The fact that he'd taken his coat off?" said McGurk.

"Yes. Because why do men take their jackets off in the house? To make themselves more comfortable, right? And usually they also take off their neckties and loosen their shirt collars at the same time."

"So?"

"Well, this guy *didn't*. He kept his necktie on. He looked just as neat and businesslike as he did out on the patio. Kind of out of place, really, in that homey setting."

All at once, McGurk seemed to relax. "Yes, well, it's their dress code."

That riveted us all.

"Huh?"

"Dress code, Chief McGurk?"

"What dress code?"

He smirked. "*Think*, men—people! It isn't only police detectives who carry guns. They don't have strict dress codes, anyway—"

"Hey! FBI!" I exclaimed.

"Correct, Officer Rockaway. Even *their* dress code might not be as strict as it used to be, but . . ." He was gazing down at the still-deserted patio with a new look in his eyes. "It could certainly explain everything. . . ."

"Explain *everything*, McGurk?" said Wanda.

"Yes. Like maybe Mr. and Mrs. Robinson are agents, and the old lady guy is a federal witness. A vital federal witness, who's being hidden until the trial. Maybe that's one of their safe houses."

A hush had now fallen over us.

I shook my head briskly. "Not so fast, McGurk. Hadn't we better look at the plain obvious facts first? Like one: the New York plates when Mr. Jones said the Robinsons had just gotten in from *California*. It just doesn't add up."

"So what?" said McGurk. "That was just their cover story."

"Well, if they *are* FBI, it's a pretty poor cover story."

"Oh, *really,* Officer Rockaway? I think it's a pretty *good* one then! It fits the supposed facts. Who'd drive four thousand miles with an old invalid lady? They'd be more likely to fly to New York and rent a car at the airport, wouldn't they?"

"Yes, but a car in *that* condition?" I glanced at Willie's notes. "All messed up, muddy. No rental company would put it on the road like that."

"Maybe they *bought* it in New York then," said Brains.

"Not in that condition, surely?" said Mari.

"Maybe it was a used car," Brains persisted.

"Come on!" I said. "Even used cars get cleaned up before being sold. *Especially* used cars."

"Well, maybe—"

"That's enough, men!" said McGurk, rapping his plaster cast. "*I* still think it's an FBI assignment."

"Well, if it is," said Wanda, "wouldn't it have Washington, D.C., plates? Or Virginia? Or Maryland? Somewhere close to FBI headquarters?"

"No, Officer Grieg! Not if it's an undercover assignment. They'd use a beat-up undercover car registered in some other state. One that nobody would think of looking at twice."

"Except me," murmured Willie. "I looked at it seven times!"

"That was different, Officer Sandowsky. You know what I mean."

We had to admit that McGurk had a point. I guess that really we all wanted it to be the kind of setup he'd been describing.

And when he began to suggest some of the things we could do to help the FBI, the last of my doubts melted away.

"Like if the gang they're trying to protect the witness from—if they get wind that the witness is here and they start casing the Mayroyd house—why, we'll be able to spot them from up here and raise the alarm!"

It was an attractive picture. Even Brains started to flush with excitement.

"Yeah!" he said. "And maybe they'll reward us with a tour of the bureau's VICAP Center for offender profiling. I'd like that!"

"I'm glad to hear you say so, Officer Bellingham," McGurk declared. "Because you, as science expert, look like you'll have a key role to play down there in the vacant lot."

11

The Hit Man Scenario

Brains's eyes widened. "What did you have in mind, McGurk?"

"Well, if that is a vital witness, and the gang does get wind of where he's being hidden—what will their first move be?"

"Send in a hit man!" said Willie, without the slightest hesitation.

"Correct, Officer Sandowsky. Almost."

"Hey!" gasped Brains. "What d'you expect *me* to do?"

"Take it easy, Officer Bellingham. I said 'almost.'"

"Right!" said Wanda. "The very first thing would be make sure the vital witness is there."

"Exactly," said McGurk. "And for that they'd send someone who knows what he really looks like. Someone also in disguise. Like pretending to be from the telephone company. Or an electric meter reader."

"Yeah," said Willie. "But when they have fingered him—*then* the hit man!"

"And that's when they'll need a place to aim from," said Wanda eagerly. "Where the hit person can get in a good clean shot."

"Like from this window!" said Willie.

McGurk's eyes popped. Then he quickly recovered.

"Very good thinking, Officer Sandowsky! You heard that, people? From here on in, no stranger is allowed in this room. No telephone guy come to check the outlet. No nurse, even, claiming to be a physiotherapist sent by Doc Baxter. Not without they're double-checked. Okay?"

There was a rustle of excited interest.

"Of course," I said, "they'd have to get past your mom first, McGurk. But—"

"I know an even better place to take a shot from, McGurk," Wanda cut in.

"Oh?"

"Sure. I've been in it myself. In the last half hour."

"The tree?" said Mari.

"You bet! If the wheelchair guy had shown himself at that window"—Wanda pointed a menacing finger— "*phut!*"

"What—what *phut*, Wanda?" said Willie.

McGurk was positively beaming. "The sound of a gun being fired. A gun with a silencer. Right, Officer Grieg?"

"You've got it, McGurk. A perfect spot. All those leaves for cover. Easy access in and out of the lot. Plenty of tall weeds to crawl through to get to the tree unseen. Ideal."

McGurk was nodding. "My thoughts exactly. Which

is why I said Officer Bellingham would have a key role. And all this cover makes it easier for him."

"Easier for me to do *what*?" said Brains.

"To fix up some device," said McGurk. "Some trip wire kind of thing that'll set off an alarm if the hit person climbs that tree or even heads for it. Okay?"

"Uh—yeah—I guess—yeah." Brains was now looking thoughtful. "It might take time to figure out all the angles and get the right equipment. . ."

"Take all the time in the world, Officer Bellingham," said McGurk. "Say until noon tomorrow."

"Well—"

"And you, officers Grieg and Yoshimura, can help him by working out the likeliest routes from the street through the weeds." McGurk turned to Brains. "You're not thinking of just *one* trip wire, are you?"

"No," said Brains. "Leave it to me, McGurk. I'll take care of that tree from every which way. I'll—"

"Hold it!" said McGurk. "Isn't that their car now?"

The vehicle was just moving along Sycamore toward East Olive.

"Yeah," Willie murmured. "That's the Olds all right."

"With only Mr. and Mrs. Robinson in it," I added. "They must have left the wheelchair guy behind."

"That doesn't seem very efficient," said Wanda. "Leaving their vital witness alone and unguarded."

"Maybe it's only for a few minutes," I said. "While they run a check on the nearby streets."

"Anyway," said McGurk, "since the wheelchair guy's on his own, now's our chance to run a doublecheck ourselves. Officer Yoshimura—" he pointed to the phone. "Call the Mayroyd house. Their number's still in the book. See who answers and what the voice sounds like."

"But who should I ask for, Chief McGurk?" asked Mari.

"Oh—one of the Mayroyd kids. Norma-Jean... Tony... And you take notes, Officer Rockaway."

And—with my ear next to Mari's—that's what I did. Take these notes:

Record of phone call to Mayroyd house, Saturday 12:15 p.m.

VOICE (after 12 rings): Yeah?

MARI: Could I speak to Tony, please?

VOICE: Who?

MARI: Tony Mayroyd.

VOICE: They don't live here no more!

HANGS UP.

"A man, definitely, Chief McGurk."

McGurk looked pleased. "Good work, Officer Yoshimura! That confirms everything we've been saying."

"And a very rough-sounding man, Chief McGurk."

"Sure. Probably a gang member himself, all set to give evidence against the others."

Wanda was the first to break the sudden hush. "Come on," she said to Mari and Brains, "let's get down there and work out just where to place the alarms."

"Huh-uh!" McGurk grunted. "Not now. Here comes the Olds again."

The couple couldn't have been gone longer than ten minutes.

"Like I said," I began, "they must have been running a quick check on the streets."

"Or picking up something for lunch," Willie murmured wistfully.

"Yes," said McGurk. "And it's time we were having ours." He turned to Wanda. "I was thinking a few sliced tomatoes might liven up the toasted cheese sandwiches..."

As we turned to leave—some heading home for our own lunches, and Wanda and Mari making for the McGurk kitchen—McGurk called Mari back.

"Before you go, Officer Yoshimura, just check the book for the local FBI number. We might need it in a hurry."

"Chief McGurk?"

"Sure. For if anything happens while the Robinsons are away from the house."

12

~

The Bellingham Early Warning System

Wanda, Brains, and Mari had plenty of chances to survey the vacant lot that afternoon. The man and woman drove off no fewer than three times, and always without the wheelchair guy.

Once again it didn't look very efficient of them. But at least the guy didn't go out into the yard, so they must have warned him to keep well out of sight. Besides, they were never absent for much more than an hour, as the following notes will testify.

They were made carefully by McGurk himself, on his leg, appropriately enough just under the local FBI numbers Mari had found for him. (Yes, numbers. Plural. One that said "office" and one that said "home." The fact that the FBI could have a *home* really gave McGurk a big kick.)

Anyway, here are those times, as he noted them down:

Sat. P.M.   1:45 – 2:35
            3:10 – 3:45
            4:05 – 5:10

When the couple came back after the second sortie, Willie said: "They must be very antsy about who might be nosing around the area."

"Oh, I don't know," said McGurk. "They're probably just going along with the house-hunting story."

We didn't say anything then. But during the couple's third absence—at four fifteen precisely—both Willie and I began to have serious doubts about McGurk's theory.

We'd been sent to the supermarket for some more grapes and oranges, while Mari and Wanda continued their survey and Brains was home gathering materials for his warning devices. And it was as we were passing the shopping plaza parking lot that Willie said, "Hey! Lookit! That's their Olds over in the end bay!"

Sure enough, it was.

"So why are you getting all worked up?" I said. "They're probably shopping for food. They've got to eat, just like anyone else."

Willie would normally have been quick to relate to that. But this time he just shrugged. "Yeah. . . well. . ."

And ten minutes later, as we wheeled our cart from the supermarket's produce section, he voiced his suspicions more openly.

"I don't see them in here anywhere."

I glanced around. It wasn't very busy in Berti's supermarket just then.

"Well, maybe they're at the realtors, getting some more house information."

"We'll check," Willie said.

He sounded very determined. I guessed it was because he'd gone to so much trouble earlier, taking those notes. It must have made it seem like his own very special duty to follow them up whenever he came across that station wagon. So we went around to the far end of the plaza to pass by W. B. Realtors' window.

Result: Negative. Just one customer, someone we'd never seen before, talking to Ms. Wilenchick.

"Satisfied, Willie?"

"I guess."

There *were* other places they could have been, like the liquor store or the pharmacy. But I kept quiet about them. Those oranges weren't getting any lighter.

"Come on," I said. "Let's get back and see how the others are making out with Brains's early warning system."

As we were going past the corner of the supermarket again, Willie clutched my arm.

"Don't look now. But there they are. In the coffee shop."

I did look right away, as a matter of fact. Automatically. But it didn't matter. The man and woman were sitting at a table next to the plate-glass window, gazing out in a different direction, almost dreamily.

"So all right," I said, moving on. "They don't seem to be in any hurry to get back. But it's no big deal."

"No?" said Willie. "Didn't you see what she had on the table in front of her?"

"A mug of coffee," I said. "Sure."

"No, as *well* as that," he insisted.

"What, then?"

"A *notebook!*" said Willie triumphantly. "Just like ours. She looked like *she'd* been taking notes, too. Wait'll we tell McGurk!"

• • •

The other three were already making their report when we arrived. McGurk looked up from a sketch Wanda was showing him, as Willie blurted out our news. McGurk didn't seem any more impressed than I'd been.

"Probably notes about some of the houses they're supposed to have been looking at." He turned back to the sketch. "You were saying, Officer Grieg? . . . "

Now since that was a very rough sketch of the vacant lot, made hurriedly, I took the trouble later to redraw it neatly for our records. After all, it did turn out to be one of the most important documents in this case and here it is, at the top of the next page.

"An intruder won't want to mess with the short grass at the edges here," Wanda explained. "Too exposed."

"But he will wish to keep to the long weeds, Chief McGurk," said Mari. "Ready to crouch down in."

"Sure, sure. . ." McGurk murmured. "So?"

"And of course he'll have his eye on the tree as the most likely lookout spot," said Wanda.

"Which is why," said Brains, "we've taken care to

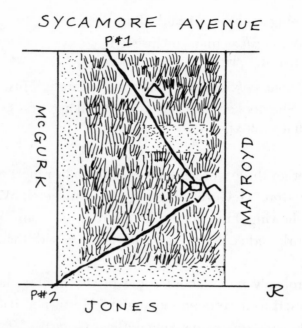

SYCAMORE AVENUE

THE BELLINGHAM EARLY WARNING
SYSTEM

offer him these two paths leading to it. *P* One and *P*
Two."

"Which we've already trampled down," said Wanda.
"As I think you can just see from up here. Number One
is the most obvious route. Straight off the street. He'd
find it hard to resist taking *that*."

"But if he is more cautious, Chief McGurk—"

"Which hit men usually are," Brains chimed in.

"—we have offered him Number Two," Mari continued.

"It would mean him sneaking along the side of the Jones's driveway," said Brains. "But at dusk or in the dark it would be a cinch. *Except*—heh, heh!—there'll be a trip wire there, on that route too."

"You mean both paths will have trip wires, huh?" McGurk said. "At the side of these triangle things?"

"Yes, but they aren't triangles, McGurk," said our science expert. "They're pyramids."

McGurk glanced up sharply. "This isn't a history project, Officer Bellingham!"

"No, not pyramids as in Pharaoh's Egypt," said Brains. "Pyramids as in Berti's supermarket. Pyramids of cans. Like the kind Joey's cousin Benny once pulled one out of the bottom of."

I winced. I could still hear the almighty racket they made as they came tumbling and rolling down.

McGurk was grinning. "Ah, yeah! I see what you're getting at, Officer Bellingham!"

"Only these won't be cans of beans," said Brains.

"But they'll make just as much noise, Chief McGurk," said Mari.

"More!" said Wanda. "Because they'll have bits of metal, nails, pebbles, and all kinds of small hard objects in them. Show him, Brains!"

Brains reached down to a tote bag he'd been keeping between his feet. "Like this old soda can. Listen."

It was rattling as he brought it up. But when he gave it a brisk shake, Mari backed away, holding her ears.

"Sorry, Mari!" Brains's face shone as he turned to McGurk. "That's just a prototype. With a few nails and screws inside. But imagine a dozen or so of these in a concealed pyramid. With a trip wire attached to a couple of the bottom ones."

"Sounds great!" said McGurk. "But what's this butterfly thing in the tree itself?"

"That's no *butterfly*! That's a 110-decibel door alarm that I'm adapting for the job. Powered by a nine-volt battery. It'll be fixed to one of the topmost branches—"

"By me," said Wanda.

"—with some string attached," Brains continued. "Crisscrossing the trunk. The intruder snags that string and *powee*! The alarm goes off and wakes the whole neighborhood!"

"Terrific, Officer Bellingham!" said McGurk. His smile faltered. "But what if a *squirrel* disturbs the string?"

"I'll be taking care of that," Brains said. "I can adjust it so it'll need a stronger tug than a squirrel's to set it off."

"So when will it be ready?" asked McGurk.

"The alarm will definitely be in working order by tomorrow afternoon," Brains declared.

"And the—uh—pyramids?"

"Well—" Brains began to polish his glasses with the hem of his shirt. "There could be some delay there."

"Delay?"

"Yeah, well, it's a question of finding the right cans," muttered Brains. "Pretty much all the same size. About six inches is ideal."

"But we're working on it, McGurk," said Wanda.

"You'd better!" said McGurk. "All of you. It's getting late now, but come tomorrow morning—nine sharp— I'll expect you to show with all the empty cans you can find."

"Of roughly the same size as this," Brains added.

"With a whole raft of small hard objects," said McGurk, giving Brains's soda-can "prototype" a joyful rattle.

13

The Building of the Pyramids

He hasn't conned you into bringing *another* bunch of get-well gifts, has he?" said Mr. McGurk, when he opened the front door the next morning.

He was in his bathrobe and rather bleary-eyed. He blinked suspiciously at our bundles as we filed into the hall—and no wonder! Five bulging plastic bags that rattled, chinked, and faintly clanked as we edged past him.

"Just some materials for an experiment, sir," said Brains.

Mr. McGurk's eyes narrowed. "Experiment? Nothing dangerous, I hope? Chemicals and stuff?"

"No, sir," said Brains. "Just acoustics. Sonics. Sound."

"Oh . . ." Mr. McGurk peeked into the top of my bag. "Cans, huh?" His face brightened. "Making a telephone system with cans joined up with tight string, right?"

"Something like that, sir," I said.

"Well, so long as you don't make too much noise . . ."

And with that he let us pass and go upstairs.

Brains hadn't been far out when he'd talked about an experiment. Constructing two pyramids of assorted cans, two feet high, isn't all that easy. As he'd already pointed out, ideally the cans had to be much the same size, five or six inches tall. And when we came to remove them from our bags, that's what they turned out to be—many of them. But it took twenty cans that size to make just one pyramid. Of the remaining twenty-seven cans only ten were of anywhere near the ideal size. Some were as tall as eight or nine inches, others as short as three.

I'd never realized before just how tin cans could vary so much and I don't think any of the others had, either—not even our science expert.

Anyway, with the building of that second pyramid, the experiment got more complicated. When an extra-tall can was used at one level, an extra-small can had to be found to even things up at the next.

"We'll just have to go empirical at this stage," said Brains.

Some of the others looked blank, but *I* knew what it meant. It meant we just had to keep trying one can after another until they fit, like pieces of a jigsaw puzzle. And this in turn meant another fancy word—*pandemonium*. Six kids with ideas of their own, mostly conflicting, with McGurk yelling at us, putting in *his* two-cents-worth every few seconds, making Willie jittery and blunder backward into the pyramid we'd already built. Only Mari and I remained anything like calm, and even she began to get nervous.

And then, when we *finally* managed to complete the

second, very rickety pyramid, what did McGurk do but reach out with the antenna, give it a flick of the wrist, and send the whole edifice crashing down!

"What's going on up there?" came Mrs. McGurk's voice from down below.

"Nothing, Mom!" McGurk called back. "Just an experiment with some empty cans."

"A *controlled* experiment!" Brains added, flushing crimson.

This seemed to satisfy Mrs. McGurk.

"What was *that* in aid of, McGurk?" said Wanda. "After all the trouble we'd taken to build it up, you go and—"

"I go and wave this antenna over it and it *collapses*! Right? Well that's what would happen out there if a *moth* went anywhere near it. So what good would that be?"

"Ah, no, wait!" said Brains. "This was just trying the cans for size. But out there they'll have their small hard objects inside them, fully operational. And those objects will not only make a louder noise. They'll also act as ballast and stabilize the pyramid. It'll take more than a moth or your—your scratching rod to knock them over then!"

Suddenly our science expert turned. "And *you* wait too, Willie!"

Willie was already reaching into his bag.

"Don't start shoving your small hard objects into the

cans yet. That's why I asked you all to keep them separate. We have to take care there's enough to go around."

So, for the next twenty minutes, peace reigned as we sorted out our small hard objects. This was doubly necessary because most of the cans—those that had contained soda or beer—had only quite small holes for drinking through. And that meant—

Well, figure it out for yourself. Here's a list of the kinds of objects we'd collected, which I typed later:

```
Beads                        Buttons (brass, bone,
Keys (luggage, etc.)            plastic)
Nails                        Lumps of solder
Screws                       Tacks (thumb)
Pebbles                      Tacks (carpet)
Ball bearings                Bottle caps
Plastic counters (from       Coffee beans
   various board games)      Sequins (from someone's
Dice                            mother's old dress)
```

Most of them were small enough, but there were some that could only be used in the cans that had open tops with lids. So we ended up with two piles of objects and two piles of cans.

Brains was just beginning to slot some nails into an old Coke can when it was Willie's turn to shout, "Wait! Hold it! All of you!"

"What's wrong, Officer Sandowsky?"

"All these soda and beer cans'll have to be rinsed out. If we don't, we'll be wasting our time hiding them in long grass."

"Why?" said McGurk.

"Because there'll be swarms of wasps hovering over them," said Willie. "And all kinds of other bugs. Looking like clouds of smoke. Drawn by the smell of beer and lemonade and stuff."

I sniffed. The air in that room *had* been getting kind of fruity.

McGurk was sniffing too. "You're right, Officer Sandowsky. Take 'em into the bathroom, people, and give them a good wash."

That took care of another twenty minutes, but after that it was all smooth sailing. By just after eleven we'd constructed two pyramids of clean cans, carefully ballasted with small hard objects, on the rug at the side of McGurk's bed.

"And now," said Brains, picking up the strings he'd already attached to some of the bottom-row cans, "we're ready to roll." He turned. "Seeing how you're the head of the Organization, McGurk, and this is your room, maybe you'd like to test the first pyramid?"

"You bet, Officer Bellingham!"

Mari had already put her hands over her ears as McGurk tugged, and one second later I was wishing I'd done the same.

Because that pyramid came down with a crash that

reminded me of a drummer coming to the end of a very loud rock number.

Then it was the second pyramid's turn. "Which I, as the scientist in charge of the experiment," said Brains, "will trigger personally."

And trigger it he did, giving the string a fierce tug and yelling, "Geronimo!"

This was the pyramid made up of uneven-sized cans, fully charged and weighted, and they didn't fall over that easily. They seemed to pause, shudder, and pause again, before—CRASH-ASH-ASH-ash-*ash*. . . . The reverberating racket made the first pyramid's fall sound like the gentle shaking of a church tambourine.

Fortunately, Mr. and Mrs. McGurk had already gone out for Sunday brunch, or the next crashing we heard would have been the sound of their footsteps pounding up the stairs. As it was, there was silence. Five seconds of stunned but blissfully happy silence. Finally, McGurk broke it, saying, "Boy, that's some early warning system, Officer Bellingham!"

Then the awed glaze faded from his eyes. "But how about the tree alarm?"

"It still needs a few final adjustments," said Brains. "I'll slip home now and make them, if it's okay by you."

"Sure," said McGurk. Then he turned to the rest of us. "Now get all this mess picked up, people, and when we're sure the coast is clear you can go set it up in the vacant lot for real!"

14

Further Strange Behavior

Well, I guess we were in luck. Mr. and Mrs. McGurk didn't get back until late afternoon, and by that time all empty cans, trip wires, and Brains's converted and finally adjusted door alarm were snugly in position.

While Wanda, Mari, and Brains were working on this, we still had to watch out for the Robinsons, of course. But once again the couple made it easy, repeating their behavior of the previous day, making no fewer than *five* short trips this time. And once again the wheelchair guy didn't appear outdoors during the others' absence.

But setting up the early warning system was only a part of the afternoon's tasks. Willie had really gotten his teeth into the mystery of all those short journeys. He kept harping on about it so much that it began to get in McGurk's hair, busy as he was, watching out for the other three down below.

"All right, Officer Sandowsky, all right!" he said at last. "If it's bugging you that much, go get your bike and patrol the streets. See if you can spot them anywhere.

You go with him, Officer Rockaway, and see he doesn't get carried away. It'll be good training."

Well, at first I wasn't one-tenth as keen as Willie, especially when he insisted on making a beeline for the shopping plaza. But, by golly, I soon changed my mind after seeing the Olds parked there. And when, a couple of minutes later, he spotted the Robinsons sitting in the coffee shop at the same table as yesterday, I began to have more respect for Willie's persistence.

"I don't see her notebook this time," he said, sounding rather disappointed.

"Maybe she's already used it," I said. "Looks like they're ready to leave."

Even as I was speaking, the man and woman got up and headed for the door. They were each carrying a brown Berti's supermarket bag, neither of which looked very full.

"Let's see where they go next," said Willie, as the couple walked over to the parking lot.

I sighed. Trying to follow a high-powered station wagon on our bikes didn't seem such a bright idea. And, sure enough, they would very soon have lost us if they'd been going far or fast. But they weren't. All they did was make one small circuit of the plaza area—out onto the main road in front, up around the back road in the rear, down the side road behind the supermarket, and onto the main road again. (See map, page 97.) Then back to the Mayroyd house.

When *we* got back, McGurk had already shouted a warning through the window and the vacant lot crew had suspended their operation and gone to join him.

This time McGurk looked more interested when we made our report. "The supermarket again, huh?" he murmured. "And why drive all the way around the plaza area like that?"

"That's the second time in two days we've seen them in the supermarket," I said.

"And who knows how many other times they went?" said Willie.

"So what?" said Brains, itching to get back to his assignment.

"So why would they buy their groceries in dribs and drabs?" McGurk said. "When they could get enough for a week in one stop?"

"Maybe the wheelchair person is one of these pushy, demanding invalids," said Wanda. "Always getting a craving for different treats and drinks and stuff, and sending people on endless errands!"

"Hey, yeah!" said Willie. "Like if he *is* a vital witness, and they're supposed to be protecting his life, maybe he wants to make sure *their* powers of observation are up to snuff."

"Of course!" said Wanda. "And that's why the woman was taking notes yesterday. I bet right now the wheelchair person's giving them a test!"

"Very funny, Officer Grieg!" growled McGurk. "You

just concentrate *your* powers of observation. Those two may decide to take a break from their endless errands and go out into the yard for a breather."

"I hope not," muttered Brains. "We still have the second pyramid and the tree alarm to fix."

He needn't have worried. It wasn't long before the Olds was on its way again.

"This'll be their third trip today," said McGurk. "Officers Sandowsky and Rockaway—"

"We're on our way!" Willie sang out, already halfway down the stairs.

We both had a very clear idea where that way would lead. That third trip and the fourth, *and* the fifth, all led to the shopping plaza again. And it *was* as if the wheelchair guy was pulling a McGurk on them. All they ever came back with were two or three small bags of stuff. Oh, yes—plus a few notes we saw the woman scribble down. Once in the coffee shop, once in the express checkout line, and twice when they got back to their car. Also, on two of those three trips, they made that same slow circuit around the back of the plaza before returning home.

And by five thirty that was it. The couple were through for the day, but by then the early warning system was already fully operational, according to Brains.

"Good work, people!" said McGurk. "And that includes you, Officers Sandowsky and Rockaway. There's probably nothing in those visits, but you never know. Meanwhile..."

He looked yearningly down at the vacant lot. It was obvious what was uppermost in his mind.

• • •

There was just one more incident before we dispersed.

Even as we were following McGurk's hungry gaze, the man and the woman strolled out onto the patio, closely followed by the wheelchair person.

Mr. Robinson was glancing around again, seemingly casually. The woman was stooping to the roses. Then suddenly she turned to the wheelchair person, who was fumbling around in a large purse, and said something to him, shaking her head impatiently.

The wheelchair person's hand froze for an instant before plunging back into the purse. But not before I saw it had been holding something long and silvery.

"Was that a *gun*?" I heard Mari whisper.

"Quiet!" murmured McGurk. "Let's see what happens now."

The woman was pointing to the poolhouse. The wheelchair person shrugged so viciously I wouldn't have been surprised if the wig had been shaken off. Then he propelled the chair toward the poolhouse, flung open the door, and, wheelspokes flashing angrily in the reddening sun, went lurching and trundling inside.

"What was all *that* about?" said Wanda.

"I think I know," said Willie. "And that wasn't a gun."

"Oh?" said Mari.

"No. I've seen this happen before. Only it was the

shed at the end of our yard, not a poolhouse. And it wasn't a wheelchair person. It was my Uncle Jake, ordered there by my Aunt Jackie. And, yes—" Willie smiled. "Look at the door!"

It was ajar, and already thick blue smoke was drifting out.

Willie sniffed. "Even from here I can smell it."

"Smell *what*, Officer Sandowsky?"

"Cigar smoke. And judging from its smell, and the size of that silver tube it was in, that's a Jamaican Macanudo. Just like my Uncle Jake smokes."

"No wonder your aunt made him smoke it out in the shed," said Wanda. "I'm beginning to catch a whiff of it myself!"

"Mrs. Robinson doesn't seem to care for it, either," said Mari. "Not even out on the patio."

"Of course not, Officer Yoshimura!" said McGurk. "It would be as big a giveaway as taking his wig off in public and waving it in the air! . . . Some sick old lady!" he continued, wrinkling his nose. "Smoking a thing like *that*!"

15

First Victim

Less than fourteen hours went by before the early warning system claimed its first victim, and the only one of us to get a grandstand view was McGurk!

Even he didn't actually see the man blunder into the pyramid near path Number One. He heard the crash, of course, and the man's shout of shock and anger. And that was when McGurk hoisted himself closer to the window and saw Mr. Robinson in his shirtsleeves, clutching a bunch of black-eyed Susans and scowling at the cans he'd sent scattering.

The time was exactly seven forty-five A.M.

But there were other witnesses: Mr. McGurk, who'd just been going to his car, at the Sycamore end of the driveway; and Mr. Braff with his twenty-year-old daughter, Nita, who'd been getting into their car in the Braff driveway opposite.

"I mean that guy's yell included a word you don't expect a respectable FBI officer to use in public," said McGurk, when he told us about the incident. "I guess he was that shook up."

The man recovered his poise, however, when Mr.

McGurk looked across and said, "Problem, sir?"

"No—it's okay," Mr. Robinson replied, switching on an apologetic smile. "I just came over to pick a few of these." He waved the black-eyed Susans. "My mother loves them. She's an invalid, you know. A shut-in. Anything to brighten up her room, poor woman!"

Mr. McGurk was sympathetic. "Well, there's plenty of those in there."

"So I realize," said Mr. Robinson. He frowned. "Also a fine old crop of cans. I just stumbled into a whole bunch of them. Some fool kids' game, perhaps."

Mr. McGurk stiffened. But he's no fink.

"Well, it won't be my kid. He's a shut-in, too, at the moment. Broken leg. Otherwise—"

"Oh, well." Mr. Robinson glanced across at the Braff car, which was now driving off. "I didn't mean to alarm the whole neighborhood. And I think I have enough now"—he gave the flowers another shake—"for her breakfast tray."

Then the man went back to the Mayroyd yard.

"About one minute later," said McGurk, "I saw the station wagon leave with just Mrs. Robinson in it, driving real fast."

"I don't buy the black-eyed Susan story," said Wanda.

"Me either," said McGurk. "*I* think he might have spotted a prowler and rushed out to investigate."

"You say he stumbled slap into the cans?" I said. "Not just snagged the trip wire?"

"Correct," said McGurk. "He didn't even *reach* the path. You can see where he flattened the weeds and made a path of his own, on the way to that pyramid."

"And he wasn't wearing a jacket?" said Wanda.

"No."

"And no sign of the shoulder holster?"

"No. Obviously he rushed out in too much of a hurry." McGurk frowned. "Not very smart for an FBI agent. . . But we all make mistakes, I guess." He brightened. "All the more reason for us to keep watch—and be prepared to assist."

"Anyway," said Brains, "he isn't likely to go triggering the *tree* alarm accidentally."

"Maybe we've gotten it all wrong," I said. "Maybe they are what they say they are."

"Baloney, Officer Rockaway!" said McGurk. "That old lady's no one's mother! That old lady is a guy!"

"And I *did* see that shoulder holster on Saturday," said Wanda.

"Okay," I said. "But maybe some of us were right the first time about that, too. Maybe the holster was to house a calculator. Maybe the wheelchair person's just their eccentric son and—"

Something down on the street seemed to have caught McGurk's attention.

"Officer Rockaway," he said, "do you think you could redraw a section of that map? Just the top half of the lot, showing the Mayroyd house and the Braff house."

"No problem," I said, already pulling out my note-book.

"With one addition," said McGurk. "That tree in the Braff yard."

He pointed to a tall, light green, fir-type tree at the side of the driveway.

"Sure," I said. "I'd have put it in before but I didn't think it had anything to do with our case."

"I didn't either. But now—well—"

"You surely don't think a hit man would use *that* tree, do you, McGurk?" I said, beginning to make the sketch. "Only a few feet from the Braffs' front windows? I mean, I can see it would give plenty of cover—"

"Be quiet a minute!" murmured McGurk. "I'm thinking."

There was silence for a few seconds. Then Wanda said, "If you're suddenly taking an interest in trees, McGurk, that one's a Thuja. It's—"

"I said I was *thinking*, Officer Grieg!" McGurk growled. "But since it bothers you, let's just say it's the tree's pyramid shape that interests *me*."

"Huh?" I grunted.

"Yes," said McGurk. "I thought it would look good to show it as a big triangle. You know—matching the small triangle marking the pyramid of cans he kicked over."

I shrugged, thinking he was being sarcastic. But I went on with the sketch anyway and this is a tidied-up version of what I produced:

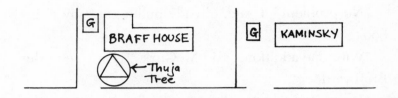

SYCAMORE AVENUE

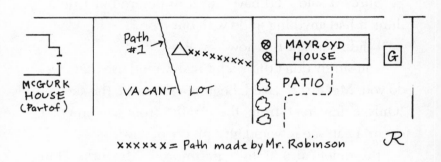

xxxxx = Path made by Mr. Robinson

"There you go, McGurk." I handed him the sketch. "I hope the tree triangle is big enough. The circle's to show the area it covers where it's all bushed out at the bottom."

McGurk studied it.

"Thanks, Officer Rockaway. Now get me a ruler. There's one in the kitchen drawer next to the dishwasher. And just check how we're doing for oranges. Your next assignment—all of you—is to go to the shopping plaza and—"

"Just for *oranges*?" said Wanda. "*All* of us?"

"No, *not* just for oranges. I want you to cover the whole plaza thoroughly, see if Mrs. Robinson's down

there now, and, if she is, check on her movements. And
then I want you all to go into the coffee shop, if the
coast is clear, and order yourselves a soda or something
and—"

"Who's paying?" asked Willie.

McGurk sighed. "It can come out of the Organization slush fund. Just one inexpensive item each. And
forget about the ruler, by the way."

He plucked Brains's antenna from under the plaster.
"I can use this instead."

"So go on, McGurk," said Wanda. "After we've all
sipped our free ice water, like a bunch of cheapskates,
then what?"

"I want you to take your time and make a note of *exactly* what's to be seen outside. If possible, from the
table the Robinsons were sitting at."

"Is this another test, Chief McGurk?"

"No, Officer Yoshimura. It is a vitally important
assignment. But—hey—that gives me an idea." He
reached for his get-well notebook and started ripping
out blank pages. "Take one each. Then you can all make
separate lists. That way you'll be on your toes and not so
likely to miss something vital."

"This *is* another test," Mari muttered as we went out,
still puzzled, but eager, leaving him to brood over the
recent sketch, with a glass of orange juice in one hand
and the scratching stick in the other.

16

~

Or Treasury Agents?

When we reached the plaza we were just in time to see the station wagon leave, driven by Mrs. Robinson.

"Well, that leaves us free to go straight to the coffee shop and get *that* part of the assignment done," said Wanda. "And I guess it's a good thing everyone'll be taking notes after all. The final list will be bigger in a shorter time."

"Oh, really?" I said coldly, wondering how *she'd* like it if I started telling her about a quicker way of climbing trees.

"Sure," she said. "It probably won't be long before they're both back here. And it wouldn't be a good idea if they came in and found us all scribbling away at their favorite table."

I guess that made sense and, before long, we'd all gotten down to work on our separate lists.

Only one other customer was in there at the time— the checkout girl, Dolly. I think she was taking her coffee break, but she cut it short when she saw us start work.

"There!" I heard her say to the person behind the

counter. "What did I tell you? They've even got *kids* taking notes now!"

I didn't think much about that remark at the time. I remembered how she'd glowered at me on one of McGurk's early observation-testing errands. Just then I was more concerned to get on with my list.

So exactly what did we see and note that morning as we looked out of that window? And what could have been of such special interest to the Robinsons on *their* visits to the coffee shop?

First, though, here's a map of the shopping plaza that I made later:

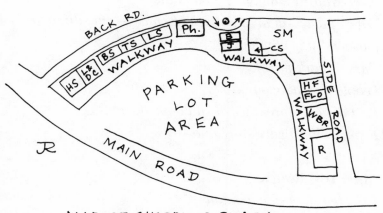

MAP OF SHOPPING PLAZA

KEY: CS = Coffee Shop
SM = Supermarket
B = Bank
☉ = Bank Drive-In
J = Jewelers
HF = Health Food Store
FLO = Florist
WBR = W. B. Realtors
R = Restaurant

Ph. = Pharmacy
LS = Liquor Store
TS = Thrift Shop
BS = Book Store
L&DC = Laundromat and Dry Cleaners
HS = Hardware Store

And the lists? Skipping the crossings-out, cola stains, and doodlings, here they are—as far as they all got.

Wanda Grieg.
C & J Jewelers side window.
Willow tree at edge of p. lot.
Branch of West Milford Savings & Loan bank.
Main door of that bank.
View of part of main parking lot.
Corner of bank's drive-in area and—

Brains Bellingham.
West Milford Savings & Loan bank.
Edge of drive-in area in back of bank—"out" direction.
Jewelers' side window.
Cars in parking lot.
People on walkway.
Part of bookstore toward end of walkway.
Front of hardware store and—

Mari Yoshimura.
C&J Jewelers side window.
Sign in window: DON'T MISS GRAND OPENING:
    "TIME OF YOUR LIFE" EXHIBITION—
    SAT. AUGUST 27.
WATCHES! CLOCKS! SUPERB GIFTS!!!
Bank and part of—

J. Rockaway.
(*Starting from the right:*)
Back road.
Section of bank drive-in area.
Bank building. (West Milford Savings & Loan.)
Bank's main door.
Narrow walkway opening between bank and C & J
  Jewelers.
Section of main plaza walkway.
Good view of parking lot.
(*Starting from far end of walkway:*)
Corner of—

Willie Sandowsky.
Ebsen's Hardware store.
Laundromat and Cleaners.
Half of Browzaway Book Store.
Corner of C & J Jewelers, like where it juts out and
  blocks off view of other stores.
Brown Olds station wagon just—

And that's where Willie broke off, gasped, "It's them!"
and we all broke off.

The Robinsons were already getting out of the car.
We didn't want them to see us busy with our lists. Besides that, we were all feeling pretty good about the
mass of details we'd noted already.

"Come on!" said Wanda. "Let's see if these details

give McGurk any new ideas. They have *me*!"

"Me, too!" said Brains.

"The jewelers and the bank," murmured Mari. "Yes. . ."

"Maybe they've had word there's going to be a robbery at one of those places," I said. "Maybe they're keeping them under observation."

"Are there two *r*'s in *arriving*?" said Willie.

"Never mind that *now*!" said Wanda. "Let's go!"

• • •

Naturally, McGurk *was* very interested, especially in the notes regarding the bank. But not in the same way.

"West Milford Savings & Loan," he said. "Isn't that where Mr. Braff works? At the head office downtown?"

"Yes," I said. "He's the deputy manager there."

"Not any longer he isn't!" said Brains. "He's been made vice president in charge of the shopping plaza branch. Has been for the past six or seven weeks."

"How do you know all that?" asked McGurk.

"Because I have an account there," said Brains, blushing.

"*You*?" exclaimed several voices.

"Well—it's for my college fund really. Mom opened it a couple of years ago, when my grandfather left me some money in his will. It's called a special education rollover trust account or something. It's—"

"All right, all right, Officer Bellingham," said McGurk. "That's all we need to know right now." He turned back to the new neighborhood sketch map, his frown deepening. Then: "How about *that*?" he murmured. "This could explain everything."

"What, McGurk?" said Wanda. "And what's so special about the map, anyway?"

"Because, Officer Grieg, the Oojah tree—"

"*Thuja* tree."

"Whatever. The important thing is that it hides the Braff driveway from anyone keeping observation from the Mayroyd house. Look . . ."

He placed his antenna on the original street map, making a straight line between the Mayroyd house and the Braff driveway. Then he did it with my latest sketch map. Sure enough, the tree came slap in the way.

"So—" I began.

"So *that's* why he could have been hurrying out into the lot. To get to where he could see the Braff driveway. Mr. Braff and Nita were getting ready to leave, remember."

"Hey, yes!" said Wanda. "And that would explain the flowers. To make it look like he'd only gone in there to pick *them*, not to snoop on the Braffs."

"Correct, Officer Grieg. There's black-eyed Susans all over the lot. He didn't need to go in there at all. He could just have reached over and picked himself as big a bunch as he wanted."

We studied the scene below, nodding. It all figured.

"But why would he want to spy on Mr. Braff?" Brains asked, rather nervously.

"Because maybe they're not FBI agents after all," said McGurk. "Maybe they're *treasury* agents. Maybe they suspect Mr. Braff of being an embezzler. Quietly stealing the bank's funds. That's why they need the wheelchair guy. To keep watch on the Braff house while they're watching out for the suspect's movements at the bank. So there's a complete twenty-four-hour surveillance."

"But why watch the bank on Saturdays and Sundays?" Brains now looked terribly worried.

"Because that's the way embezzlers operate," said McGurk. "They have to keep going to the office *outside* regular working hours. So there's no one else around to see them falsify the records. That's probably why the Robinsons spent so much time down there on Saturday and Sunday. Probably checking on the times of his visits to the bank."

"Of course!" I said. "And it explains why they kept making those circuits around the back of the plaza on Sunday, when Willie and I followed them."

"Oh?" said Willie, suddenly alert.

"Yes," I said. "From the coffee shop you can only see *part* of the bank's drive-in area, like I pointed out in my notes."

"And I in mine," said Wanda.

"Mine, too," said Brains, still looking very unhappy.

"So what?" said Willie.

"So the Robinsons wanted to get a better view of the

bank's drive-in area to check if Mr. Braff's car was parked there."

"Good thinking, Officer Rockaway!" said McGurk. "Like in that Lieutenant Carmichael episode when— hey! Where are you going, Officer Bellingham?"

"Home," said Brains. "Right now. So Mom can start transferring my account immediately, before—"

"Stay where you are! It's only a hunch at this stage. It's just that it makes a common link—watching house, watching office. It *could* be a coincidence. But we'll keep it in mind from now on, people!"

• • •

We spent the rest of the day keeping an eye on the Robinsons' movements. They didn't make so many trips to the plaza this time. Instead, they seemed to be taking it easy, mainly lounging around on the patio.

The wheelchair guy didn't show at all. This made McGurk remember what he'd said about the guy being assigned to keep watch from the front.

"Maybe from an upstairs window," he added.

So from time to time he had us go along the street, checking—usually in ones and twos.

"But if he *is* keeping watch," said Wanda, "won't it make him suspicious? Us gaping up at the windows?"

"Not if you do it the way you've been trained, Officer Grieg. Not stopping or slowing down. Observing out of the corners of your eyes. Concentrating on one window only, each time."

Well, that sounds okay in theory. But not out there on the street, with screens making it difficult to see anything inside, even when the drapes weren't drawn.

When it was Willie's and my turn, concentrating on the second-floor window far right, I thought I detected a slight movement. But since the window was open a crack, I guessed the curtain had probably been stirred by the breeze.

Willie said *he* hadn't seen the movement, that he must have had his eyes closed.

"Eyes *closed*?" I said. "Boy, McGurk's going to dump on *you*!"

"Yeah, well, I was sniffing. Concentrating on my sense of smell. I figured that the wheelchair guy wouldn't be able to resist a puff at his cigar every once in a while. I know my Uncle Jake wouldn't."

"So?" I said. "Did you smell anything?"

"Well—uh—no. I wasn't quite sure, but. . . no. If he *was* up there he wasn't smoking at that moment. I *think*. . ."

He was looking worried, probably wondering if his marvelous sense of smell was deserting him.

Yes, buster! I thought. That's what comes of muscling in on another expert's territory. Thinking you're a star note taker. You neglect your own true talent and before you know what's happened you've lost it for good!

17

~

Dolly's Revelation
–and More from Mr. Jones

Three tremendously important developments took place the next day, Tuesday.

The first was that we were told not to report to our new HQ until after lunch. It was the morning for Doc Baxter to give McGurk his first real checkup since leaving the hospital. Nothing tremendous about that? Just wait. You'll see...

The second was what I found out that morning. Some of the others had gone shopping for back-to-school stuff. Some had been detailed to do various chores connected with their own homes. One of mine was to pick up some dry cleaning at the shopping plaza.

But naturally, when I saw the Olds station wagon parked there, I couldn't resist looking in at the coffee shop to see if the Robinsons were there. They weren't, but when I spotted them just about to enter the bank, I decided to buy myself a Coke and wait and see how long they took.

It was busy, but luckily I was able to get a table near the window, and I had just pulled out my notebook when a voice said:

"You again? With the notes. What is this? Some kinda contest?"

It was the checkout person, Dolly, holding a mug of coffee.

"Mind if I join you?"

I shook my head and said, "Contest?"

"Yeah. These notes I'm always seeing you making."

"Well. . . It's kind of. . . well. . . you know."

"No, I *don't* know," she said. "But I have a pretty good idea. I see the others doing it all the time."

"Others?" I said.

"Yes," said Dolly, looking beyond me. "Those two especially. Just coming out of the bank."

I looked out, startled. Sure enough, there they were—the Robinson couple. And this time they *did* notice me. The woman stared straight at my notebook, nudged the man and said something. Then he looked, and if he *was* an FBI agent his training hadn't been as good as ours. No covert eye-corner routine with him. He actually made direct eye contact. Only one quick suspicious glare, but it left me feeling cold all down my back.

"I can see they're no friends of yours, anyway," said Dolly.

"You say you've seen them taking notes?"

"Sure. They're always doing it. In the store and in here. I thought at first they were just doing some comparison shopping. Checking prices and stuff. But now I think it's more like they're counting customers. I just can't be sure. Is that what you're doing? Counting customers?"

"No," I said. "Just a vacation assignment—kind of."

"Well, that's what *they* seem to be doing. Also counting how many people pass by without coming in. Usually in the mornings, but other times, too."

"Is that all they do?"

"Well, no. They buy stuff. Mostly under ten items. Usually, it's only single people in a hurry who use the express line. But they're not single and they never seem in a hurry. In the mornings it's just fresh fish, as soon as the Boston truck gets in. Every morning for weeks now."

"*Weeks*? But—"

"But I think it's just an excuse to come snooping. The creeps!"

And that's when Dolly got it off her chest. *Her* theory was that the store was about to be taken over by a big supermarket chain, and that the Robinsons were a couple of market researchers, checking up on how much business Berti's was doing. Also checking on how efficient and polite the clerks were. Dolly was wondering just how safe her job was!

Well, that gives us yet another possible explanation for the Robinsons' strange behavior, I thought. But what was the question I was going to ask her?

As I stared at that blank notebook page, I couldn't

remember at first, and she'd already returned to her checkout duties by the time it came back to me.

Of course! She'd said *weeks*! The Robinsons had come to buy fish every morning for *weeks*. Yet they'd arrived in town only four or five days ago!

Then I shrugged. Probably she'd been exaggerating. Probably, in her growing anxiety, it had *seemed* like weeks. So I got on with my other errands without bothering to check further.

And boy, was *that* a mistake!

• • •

McGurk was looking very eager when we all turned up after lunch. Doc Baxter had told him he was doing fine and could start moving around on his crutches more—though not up and down the stairs yet. But that wasn't the reason for his surge of eagerness.

"There's been another development!" he said.

"What kind?" asked Brains. "Has the second pile of cans been triggered?"

"No. But the Robinson guy's had a run-in with Mr. Jones."

We stared.

"What about?" said Wanda.

"How would I know?" said McGurk. "It happened while Doc Baxter was examining me."

"Well, how do you know it was a run-in?" I said.

"The way they were acting, with Mr. Robinson waving his arms about. He was in the vacant lot. Mr. Jones looked like he'd been about to go over himself and trim that strip of weeds, but Mr. Robinson was ordering him to keep out. That's the way it looked, anyway."

"So?"

"So I want you, Officer Rockaway, to go down and ask Mr. Jones if it's anything to do with us. The guy kept pointing to where he'd stumbled into the cans. Once, he even looked up toward this window and said something."

"Oh, boy!" I groaned. "I think he's beginning to suspect us of keeping watch on him!"

I described the way the couple had scowled at me earlier, and I was about to tell them of Dolly's theory, but McGurk cut me short.

"Later, Officer Rockaway. I can hear Mr. Jones's mower now. See what you can find out."

"I'll go, too!" said Willie, snatching up McGurk's get-well notebook again.

Mr. Jones was working on the grass at the front. He switched off the power and said, "Hi! I've been hoping I might see some of you before long."

"Sir?"

"Yes. To give you a warning. Keep out of that vacant lot. The new people are getting very antsy about it."

"Is that a fact, sir?" said Willie.

"Yes. The guy even ordered *me* out this morning. And I was only going to cut down some of the weeds. You'd think he'd look on it as a favor—but not this guy!"

He said, 'We're thinking of buying the Mayroyd house and this lot goes with it. Our lawyer says it would complicate the deal if neighbors made a habit of coming in and doing what they like. So just keep out!' That's what he said, and he didn't say please!"

"Oh, boy!" I murmured.

"Yeah!" Mr. Jones continued. "He also said, 'It's bad enough having kids coming in and out!' Meaning you guys, obviously."

"But what's with this *buying* the place?" I said. "I thought the Mayroyds were coming back."

"That's what I thought, too. So I gave Myra Wilenchick a call. She said she hadn't heard about the Robinsons thinking of buying the place, but she wasn't surprised. They'd been so red-hot keen to rent it after being so hard to please with their earlier rental."

"*Earlier* rental?"

"Oh, yes. They'd already been in the area four weeks. In another rental across town."

This stunned me. "I thought you told me they'd only just arrived, Mr. Jones?"

"In this *neighborhood* is what I said, Joey. Anyway, according to Myra, they finally decided the other neighborhood wouldn't do, and wasn't there something they could rent over here. Like the Mayroyd house they'd seen on the W. B. Realtors' list. Myra said yes, but not for a period of less than three months and at a much higher rent. . . What's the problem, Willie?"

Willie was looking around, sniffing. Some notetaker!

"Never mind him, Mr. Jones," I said. "Go on with what you were saying."

"Well, that didn't put the Robinsons off. Myra says they paid the whole three months' rent in advance, plus a big deposit, in *cash*. So if they're *that* keen on the house—" Mr. Jones shrugged.

I nodded. I was feeling impatient to get back. I mean, this verified what Dolly had told me!

But Willie was still sniffing.

"What's wrong, son?" said Mr. Jones. "You smelling drains?"

"Fish. Raw fish. Going off."

Mr. Jones's eyes widened. "Hey, that's some nose you've got! I can't smell it here, but it's sure strong enough around the back."

"Oh?" I said.

"Yeah. And I've half a mind to tell the guy to do something about it."

"Tell him what?"

"To either get his garbage disposal fixed or move that stinking garbage can back near his own house. Yeah! That's what he was doing—moving it to this end—when he had the gall to come over into the lot and tell me to keep out."

"Come on, Willie," I said. "Let's get back."

"But I haven't made any notes yet!"

"Your sense of smell has just done the work of twenty

pages full of notes," I said. "It's just proved that the Robinsons' trips to the supermarket are only a cover!"

• • •

McGurk was impressed. "It's obvious," he said, when we'd reported back and I'd added what Dolly had told me. "We've been barking up the wrong trees, people!"

His eyes were glowing. He looked more positive than he had all along. He was out of bed and pacing—well, lurching on his crutches—up and down.

"What wrong trees, McGurk?" asked Wanda.

"Like for instance about being FBI agents with a vital witness," he said. "If they'd spotted someone snooping around that earlier rented house, they'd have moved out of this town altogether."

"Well, it was *you* who said they were FBI agents," Wanda began.

"And *treasury* agents," McGurk said, ignoring the interruption. "If they were investigating Mr. Braff for embezzlement, why didn't they come to the Mayroyd house straightaway, weeks ago?"

"But it was you who said that, too, Chief McGurk. About—"

"I know. But that was before we got this new information."

"I always *thought* Mr. Braff wasn't a crook," said Brains, looking vastly relieved all at once.

"So where does that leave us?" said Wanda. "Maybe Dolly's right. Maybe they're just market researchers."

"Not so, Officer Grieg. It doesn't explain the wheel-chair guy—and don't give me that garbage about him being their eccentric son again." He frowned. "And talking about garbage, how did Mr. Jones know that the Mayroyd disposal is broken?"

I shrugged. "Maybe the Robinson guy mentioned it. Or maybe Mr. Jones knew already."

"Or maybe he just *assumed* it," said Willie. "Because of the stink."

McGurk nodded. "Maybe. But it tells us something else important, too."

"What's that?" I asked.

"That those people either can't afford a plumber or—what's more likely—they can't risk having strangers coming into their house."

"Or the yard," said Mari, thoughtfully.

"So what's your theory *now*, McGurk?" said Wanda.

"What it was the minute I saw the guy's bald head. That something crooked's going on."

"So why all the fancy stuff about FBI and treasury agents?"

He resumed his clumping and lurching. "Because I was feeling soft, I guess. Wanting to give them the benefit of the doubt. It must have been the medication."

"What medication?" asked Brains.

"The stuff they've been giving me ever since I was in the hospital. Pills to quiet me down, stop me fussing."

"They could have fooled *me*!" murmured Wanda.

"Well, now Doc Baxter's canceled that stuff. And it's already wearing off." McGurk stopped and shook his left crutch at the window. "Those creeps are *crooks*, people! Got to be." He resumed the pacing. "And they're planning a big job of some kind."

"Yeah, the bank or the jewelers," said Wanda, thoughtfully.

"Perhaps both," said Mari.

"Oh, the jewelers would be *my* guess!" said Brains.

"Whatever," said McGurk. "But from now on, people, we intensify our surveillance. Hey—and be extra cautious! Remember what Mr. Jones said. They're getting very touchy about intruders in the vacant lot. Especially kids!"

18

~

The Midnight Alarm

Those creeps are *crooks*, people!"

It was just as if the Robinsons had heard McGurk's declaration, they kept such a low profile after that.

None of them appeared in the Mayroyd yard that afternoon. No curtains stirred when we made our (very cautious) patrols along Sycamore. And although the station wagon wasn't in the driveway or the garage (the doors had been left open), it wasn't in the plaza parking lot, either, when we went to look. Only the facts that McGurk saw the station wagon return in the evening and lights begin to appear in the Mayroyd windows kept us from thinking the trio had cleared out completely.

Even on Wednesday we saw very little of them.

When we went along to the plaza midmorning the station wagon was there all right. But—no Robinsons.

We looked for them everywhere: in the supermarket, the coffee shop, the pharmacy, the bank, the jewelers. We split up in pairs and searched carefully, systematically: hardware store, laundromat, bookstore. Nothing. Thrift shop, liquor store, health-food store, florists. The same. We prowled around the realtors and the Willow-

ware Restaurant, peeking in at the windows, but
again—no Robinsons.

Yet the station wagon remained in the parking lot,
empty.

"They seem to have vanished completely," said
Wanda, shortly before twelve o'clock. "Just dumped the
station wagon and disappeared!"

"So what now?" said Willie. "Go home for lunch?"

"I'll call McGurk and inform him of the situation," I
said, making for the pharmacy pay phone.

Our leader was very intrigued.

"Well, there's no sign of them here," he said. "You
sure it's *the* station wagon?"

"Positive."

"You'd better stick around then and keep looking."

"What about lunch?"

"You'll just have to take it in turns to go home," he
said. "So long as one of you keeps the car under observation."

So that's what we did, and it wasn't until one forty-
five that the couple turned up at last.

Not on foot, though. No, sir! But in a shiny black
Ford Escort that slid into the parking slot next to the
station wagon.

"Do you see what *I* see?" said Wanda, as the couple
got out.

"The station wagon musta broke down," said Willie.

"Oh, no, it hasn't!" said Brains, as the couple strolled

across to the Olds, got in, and started the engine.

"Well, how about *that*?" murmured Wanda, watching them drive off.

She looked completely baffled. So did McGurk when we told him about the Ford.

"But I saw them arrive home in the station wagon," he said. "About ten minutes ago. It must be parked in the driveway."

"So it is," I said. "But what we saw, we saw. They now have what looks like a nearly new Ford as well. Parked at the plaza."

"At least we know where they bought it," said Brains.

"Or rented it," said Mari.

"Oh?" said McGurk.

"Yes." I consulted my notebook, where I'd noted the car's number and other details. "Wilbur's Garage. Just across the road from the plaza. It has their logo on the back window."

"The Robinsons must have made their deal earlier," said Wanda. "Before we got there. Then took it for a spin."

"Some spin!" said McGurk. "If it lasted all morning."

"Yes, well, that's another puzzle." I glanced at my notes again. "We checked the mileage."

"*My* idea," said Brains.

"A little over three thousand," I said. "Which didn't tell us much except that the car wasn't as brand new as it looked."

"But the trip odometer had clocked only twenty-seven miles," said Brains.

"Correct," I said. "Not very far, to say it took them nearly four hours."

"Huh!" grunted McGurk. "That *is* a puzzle!"

"And why didn't they bring it back to the house?" said Mari. "That is another puzzle."

"Very fishy!" was all McGurk said to that. "Very, *very* fishy!"

• • •

When we reported for duty the next morning, I expected our first assignment would be to go to the shopping plaza and see if the Ford was still there.

But McGurk obviously had something even more pressing on his mind. He was resting heavily on his crutches and scowling down at something on the bed.

"What's wrong, McGurk?" asked Wanda. "And why did your mom look so tight-lipped when she let us in?"

I nodded. Mrs. McGurk hadn't been her usual self. She looked pale and drawn, like she'd been up half the night, and she'd answered my bright "Good morning, ma'am!" with a grim "It better be!"

"Wrong? *That's* what's wrong!" McGurk stabbed his left crutch at the jumble of articles on the bed: his get-well notebook, the scratching stick, Wanda's binoculars, and—

"The alarm!" yelped Brains. "What's it doing *there*?"

I myself hadn't recognized that round flat plastic disc

at first. But Brains was in no doubt. That door alarm had been at the very heart of his early warning system, lashed to the top of the crab tree with green gardening string.

A piece of that string was still attached to it.

"What it's doing here is"—McGurk swallowed hard—"it went off last night."

"Huh? *When?*"

"Just before midnight. Didn't any of you hear it?"

We shook our heads—stunned.

"Everyone around *here* did," said McGurk, bitterly. "Lights went on in bedroom windows. People were sticking their heads out and yelling. Mr. Jones came out with a spotlight. And—"

"Did you *see* the intruder?" asked Wanda.

"Yes," said McGurk. "Halfway down the tree already. A raccoon. And by this time the Robinson guy had come out in his bathrobe with *his* spotlight and had another run-in with Mr. Jones."

"He did?" said Brains.

"Yes. Mr. Jones said, 'This is what happens when people stuff their garbage cans with raw fish. Attracting all the raccoons from miles around!' Then Mr. Robinson snapped right back, 'But it has a raccoon-proof lid. Look, you old fool, it's still intact!' Then he swung his light back onto the tree. 'And what's a security alarm doing up a tree anyway?' he said. It was dangling loose, from a branch. It had stopped squawking by now. 'Did *you* put it there?' he said to Mr. Jones. Very loud and very ugly." McGurk paused. "I mean, being a crook he *would* be very rattled, wouldn't he?"

"Go on, McGurk," I urged. "What did Mr. Jones say to that?"

"He only got as far as, 'Now you see here, sir—'" McGurk gulped again. "Then another flashlight came on the scene. My dad's. He'd gone down to where our yard joins the Jones yard and the vacant lot, to get a closer look. Then—then he stepped over into the lot and he—he began marching toward the crab tree. . ."

"Oh, no!" cried Mari.

McGurk looked glum. "You've got it, Officer Yoshimura. He tripped the second pile of cans!"

We stared at him.

"Then what, McGurk?" Wanda whispered.

"Well, after he'd gotten over the shock, he apologized to the other two. Said he now had a purr-ity good idea what it was all about. That his son and his son's friends must have been conducting an experiment concerning the nighttime habits of wild animals. That one of the girls was a nature freak and one of the guys was nuts about scientific devices. 'But leave the rest to me, gentlemen,' he said. 'I'll see it never happens again.'"

"Could you hear all this?" I said.

"No," muttered McGurk. "The madder my father gets, the quieter he talks. But don't worry. He told me *all* about it, first thing this morning. Which is what *this* is doing here."

He stirred the alarm with his crutch.

"Be careful, McGurk!" said Brains.

"Oh, it won't go off again. He confiscated the battery."

"And what did *you* say?" I asked.

"I had to admit it," McGurk said. "Told him it *was* an experiment, yes. An experiment in scaring off nocturnal intruders. My dad thought I meant raccoons. I only hope the Robinsons thought that, too . . . What's wrong, Officer Grieg?"

Wanda's sharp cry had made us all turn. She'd been surveying the scene of last night's drama, but all at once she'd dropped the binoculars like they were red hot.

"*What*, Officer Grieg?"

"Don't—don't look now," said Wanda, "but I just noticed a movement beyond the crab tree and—oh, boy!"

"And *what*, Officer Grieg?"

"Suddenly I found myself staring into *another* pair of binoculars! Down there, at the edge of the patio. The Robinson man's—*trained on this window!*"

19

The Surprise Visitor

That afternoon, we had a visitor. . . .

It was about two P.M. Mari had created a stir by bringing along that morning's *Gazette*. She'd folded it open at an item that had caught her eye when she'd gone home for lunch.

Here's a copy:

PRICELESS CLOCK FOR LOCAL DISPLAY—ONCE OWNED BY FRENCH QUEEN

Centerpiece of the "Time of Your Life" exhibition, opening Saturday at C & J Jewelers in the Willow Park shopping plaza, will be one of the world's most valuable mantel clocks. The carved figures on its richly detailed gilded bronze case depict "The Triumph of True Love Over Time," and it is said to have once belonged to Queen Marie Antoinette of France.

Special Security Precautions

The exhibition, which is going on a three-month tour of C & J stores throughout the Northeast region, will be here for one week only and is expected to attract wide attention. Special security precautions have been taken, and the clock will be displayed in a bullet-proof glass case. This will allow the public to get close enough to admire its delicate workmanship without endangering it in any way.

"I think *this* may be their target," said Mari. "Not the bank."

"Hey, yes!" said Brains.

"Hmm!" murmured McGurk. "Maybe you're right, Officer Yoshimura. Which means they could be making their move as early as Saturday." He frowned. "Then again, maybe the bank does come into it. Maybe it's part of the special precautions to keep the clock in the bank's strong room overnight. It's only next door and—"

That was when the doorbell rang and we heard Mrs. McGurk say, "Oh, hello, Mr. Robinson! This *is* a surprise. I hope you managed to get some sleep last night, after—"

"Sure, no problem, ma'am. And to show there's no ill feeling I've brought along a little get-well gift for your son."

"Oh, but—come in, do!"

By now we were all straining our ears.

"It's from my mother, really," the man was saying. "Maybe you've seen her out in the yard—the old lady in the wheelchair. Being a shut-in herself—poor, dear, patient old soul—she felt so sorry for the kid she asked me to give him this and tell him not to give up hope. May I?"

"Of course!" said Mrs. McGurk. "Come this way."

As we heard their footsteps on the stairs, McGurk unfroze. He rapidly lurched to the bed and lay down.

"Careful, people!" he whispered. "Leave all the talking to me!"

"I've brought up a visitor, Jack," Mrs. McGurk announced. "Mr. Robinson, our new neighbor. In spite of last night, his mother—"

"Think no more about it!" said Mr. Robinson. "Hi!" he said, including us all in one broad smile. "So you're the nature detectives!" His eyes, like his smile, seemed to be taking in everything. Then he held out a bulging paper bag. "From my mother—one shut-in to another!"

"Gee, she shouldna!" murmured McGurk, gingerly withdrawing a huge family-sized tub of chocolate-chip ice cream.

"My! Your favorite, too!" said Mrs. McGurk, as she took the tub from McGurk and began to read its label.

The visitor smiled; McGurk goggled.

The man was smiling at Mrs. McGurk. He didn't see McGurk's expression of perplexity and alarm. *He* was staring at Brains, just behind the man—and no wonder!

At first I thought our science expert was being attacked by a wasp or a deer fly or something. His face was purple and his eyes were popping as he flung his arms about—to the side, up, down, across. Suddenly, Mrs. McGurk noticed him, too.

"Why, what's wrong, Gerald?"

"A—uh—nothing! I—I—" Brains stuttered. By now,

the visitor had turned to look at him, eyes narrowed and suspicious. "Just a touch of cramp!" said Brains, beginning to rub his left arm vigorously, his face turning from purple to crimson.

Then McGurk's eyes gleamed and he said, "It must be all that semaphore you've been practicing."

"Huh? Yes, yes, you're right, McGurk," said Brains. "Semaphore, yes. That's *exactly* what must have caused it!"

And so it was—in a way. As Brains explained later, he'd actually been trying to semaphore a warning about the ice cream:

BEWARE
OF
POISON!

Whether he was doing it right or not, I couldn't say. I guess he *had* been practicing a lot in the last few days, at that. Learning the code by heart. On the other hand, knowing Brains and his semaphore messages, it could just as well have come out as a warning to Robinson himself:

BEWARE
OF
PRISON!

But the fact that Brains had been trying to semaphore *anything* behind the man's back had been

enough for McGurk. He'd very quickly *guessed* what
the message must have been about.

"I'll go get some spoons," said Mrs. McGurk.

"No, that's okay, Mom," said McGurk, hurriedly.
"Just put it in the refrigerator and we'll eat it later."

The man didn't seem to hear Brains's deep sigh of relief.

"Anyway, Jack," he said, "*my* mother wants you to
know how much she sympathizes with you."

His eyes were still roving: from the window to the
bed, then over the binoculars, the scratching stick, and
the notebook at McGurk's side. I was glad to see that the
notebook was closed. It sure wouldn't have done for him
to see the number of his own station wagon scrawled
there, in Willie's messy notes! I was also relieved to see
that Mari had refolded the *Gazette* with the priceless
clock item out of sight.

"Oh, dear! There just isn't room in this refrigerator,"
said Mrs. McGurk. "I'd better take the ice cream down
to the freezer before it starts to melt."

The man seemed to relax even more when Mrs.
McGurk left the room. *We* certainly didn't when we
heard his next words.

"Autographs, huh?"

He was gazing down at McGurk's leg.

"Yes, sir," said McGurk, rapidly covering as much as
possible with his dressing gown.

I caught my breath. Had he left anything exposed that might arouse the man's suspicions?

"Would you like to autograph it yourself, sir?" McGurk added.

Now I have to hand it to McGurk here. As he said later, "I guessed if he really was a crook, that would be the last thing he'd want to do—sign his name in front of witnesses."

And McGurk's instinct was right. The man took a step back. "No—uh—I'd love to. But I have this crazy superstition. Sign someone's plaster cast and before the year's out you'll be in plaster yourself." He glanced at our faces and laughed. "It's purely a personal thing. It won't apply to *you* guys. So long as you're careful and watch your own steps. Especially when you climb trees!"

Our smiles faded, even as his broadened.

"But say—what's *this*?" He was staring at one of the few stretches of plaster left exposed. "Phone numbers? *Office* and *Home*?"

I took a quick, anxious peek. Originally, McGurk had headed that note like this:

Local Fo Bo Io Numbers

But I'd warned him that it might have his mother asking awkward questions. So he'd obliterated that heading by writing the word *apple* over it several times. Like this:

"*Secret* phone numbers, too," said the man, still peering.

McGurk's face was crimson. "Well—uh—yes, sir. They—they're my girlfriend's!"

"My!" The man's grin broadened further. "At *your* age! You have a girlfriend who works in an office?"

"Oh—only part time," McGurk said hurriedly. "She's in my class at school. She helps out in her father's office during vacations."

The man was looking at our faces. Mostly they wore uneasy, strained expressions, while Mari's was very sad.

I thought I'd better help out, but fast!

"Sure. It's a family business." Then I turned. "But I thought you'd have gotten Sandra's phone numbers by heart, McGurk?"

As soon as I said this, I could have bitten my tongue off. For some reason that was the only girl's name I could think of right then. The name of McGurk's archenemy, Sandra Ennis!

"Sandra, huh?" murmured the man. "That's a pretty name." He swung around. "Are *you* Sandra?"

"Give me a break!" Wanda blurted it out, but I guess it gave the story a ring of truth. Robinson seemed to relax. He winked. "It looks like there's some strong rivalry for your affections, Jack!"

This time, Wanda looked like throwing up on the spot. And that didn't do any harm, either.

Anyway, just then Mrs. McGurk came back and asked the visitor if he'd like a coffee and he thanked her and said no, he had to attend to some urgent business back home.

• • •

"What did you go and use *that* name for?" said McGurk, once we were on our own. "I was all set to say Fiona Baines Irwin."

Wanda looked up sharply. "Who's *she*?"

"No one," said McGurk. "But it would have accounted for the initials if he'd spotted them through all this scrawl." He looked anxiously at our voice expert. "But how about *him*, Officer Yoshimura? All that stuff about his mother—"

"Lying through his teeth, Chief McGurk . . . Just as you were," Mari added sorrowfully.

"Huh! What else could I do? Do you think he noticed it, though?"

"Well, I'm not sure," said Mari. "He sounded very relieved when he said that about Wanda being Sandra's rival. You know, about—"

"All right, all right, Officer Yoshimura! So long as he bought it."

"Yes! Drop the subject, Mari." Wanda turned. "So

now we've survived *that*, McGurk, what next?"

"We still keep up our surveillance, but very, very cautiously. Concentrating on the fact that the clock looks like their target and Saturday the day they'll make their move. Which means that for the next thirty-six hours they'll be increasing *their* surveillance on the C & J store and—"

"There they go now!" said Willie.

We rushed to the window. The station wagon was heading off in the direction of the shopping plaza.

"Officers Rockaway and—"

"We're on our way!" said Willie, jumping the gun again.

20

Blueprint for a Holdup

We were just in time to see the Ford move out of the parking lot with Robinson at the wheel, closely followed by his wife in the station wagon.

"They must be taking the Ford back to the Mayroyd house after all," said Willie.

"Huh-uh!" I murmured, as the cars turned into the road. "Opposite direction. Come on—we'd better let McGurk know right away."

McGurk was as puzzled as the rest of us.

"Maybe they're taking the Ford for another test drive," said Brains.

"So why didn't they *both* get in?" I said. "And leave the station wagon in the parking lot, like yesterday?"

We were still wrestling with the problem when McGurk suddenly stopped in the middle of his pacing. "Here's the station wagon now! Just turning into the Mayroyd driveway."

"Who was driving?" I said.

"I'm not sure," said McGurk. "I just wasn't ready for it."

"Well, there's no sign of the Ford," said Brains.

"No," said McGurk. "I got the impression they were both in the station wagon. They probably left the Ford in the parking lot again. Officer Rockaway, why don't you go take another look? On your own, this time."

"Huh?" grunted Willie, looking hurt.

"Yes," said McGurk. "Just one of you will be less conspicuous. They could be testing us. Seeing if we're following every move they make. So keep out of sight, Officer Rockaway. Slip over the fence onto East Olive and take the long way around from there."

Somewhat reluctantly, I did all that. But when I reached the shopping plaza my mood very quickly changed and I legged it back to HQ as fast as possible.

"Guess what!" I gasped.

The others were close to the window. They turned, startled.

"What?" said McGurk.

"The Ford *isn't* parked at the plaza!"

"Where is it, then?" said Willie.

"How would *I* know?" I said. "Maybe your impression was wrong, McGurk. Maybe only *one* of them was in the station wagon when it came back, and the other's still out there, driving around in. . ."

I trailed off. McGurk was shaking his head and motioning toward the window with his crutch. I went across. Both the man and the woman were out on the patio, taking the air.

"Wherever the Ford is," said McGurk, "they can't

have driven it very far. As to where they left it this time, I don't know. But I've now got a very strong feeling they might be making their move earlier than Saturday. Maybe the guy did spot something to cause him to speed up their plans, after all."

"But *what*?" I said, looking around anxiously.

The get-well notebook with Willie's notes about the station wagon was still closed. Mari's copy of the *Gazette* was still folded with the clock item well out of sight. Could it have been the boxes of files, I wondered, with their telltale labels about Mysteries Solved and Latest Mystery, Records and Clues? But then the man had called us "nature detectives," so labels like that shouldn't have given him any problems.

"I don't know," said McGurk, frowning down at his leg, deep in thought. Then suddenly he stiffened. "Hey, wait! What if he memorized one of these numbers and dialed it as soon as he got home? Just as a check? I know *I* would have!"

Mari was nodding vigorously. "That would explain why he left in such a hurry, Chief McGurk. Before the number slipped out of his mind."

Wanda gasped. "Oh, gosh! Yes! And when he hears the reply, 'FBI. How may we help you?'—the guy flips."

"Not so fast, Officer Grieg. You've just seen him in action in this room, haven't you? We're dealing here with one very smooth professional operator. So no. All he does when he hears that reply is quietly, coolly, put down the receiver and get to work straightaway on a new timetable, bringing the whole thing forward!"

"Should we call the police, Chief McGurk?" asked Mari.

"What? And say we suspect some new neighbors of planning to steal a clock? Because we think an old lady is really a bald guy with a long white wig? Because they buy fresh fish every day just to dump it in a garbage can? Can you imagine what Lieutenant Kaspar would say to *that*?"

"But—"

"No," said McGurk firmly. "We need something the cops won't be able to shrug off. And I think I know what . . ."

"What, McGurk?" Willie whispered.

"The way I see it," said McGurk, "the wheelchair guy has a key part in their plan, right?"

"Sure," I said. "To keep watch from the house, while—"

"*Partly* that, yes, Officer Rockaway. But mainly, since it's either a bank or a jewelers they're aiming to hold up, that guy's going to be their decoy. Harmless old lady in a wheelchair. Pushed into that store or bank by a re-spectable-looking middle-aged couple. Who's going to suspect *them* of intending to do anything bad?"

McGurk was sitting on the edge of the bed with the dressing gown wrapped around him. "So, in they go, with everybody minding their own business, then—

bam!" He suddenly pulled his scratching stick from under the gown and pointed it ceilingward. "The harmless old lady pulls a shotgun from under her dress and fires at the ceiling and the Robinson guy shouts, 'This is a stickup! Everybody on the floor!' and—well—see what I mean?"

We nodded, some of us still in shock after the sudden violence of the picture he'd drawn—that blueprint for a holdup.

"So—" I began.

"So we wait until we see the wheelchair guy leaving the house with them, and *then* we call the cops, alerting them to get down to both the jewelers and the bank. And that'll probably be in the morning, as soon as they're open."

"Are you *sure*, McGurk?" asked Wanda.

"Pretty sure," said McGurk. "That's been their favorite time for casing the plaza area. Checking how many people are around when they've been buying fish."

Mari nodded. "Not so many as later in the day, right, Chief McGurk?"

"Correct, Officer Yoshimura. Which makes it the best time for them to strike. And that's why I want you all here *early* tomorrow, people."

"But the exhibition won't be open until Saturday," said Wanda, "and the clock—"

"The clock will already be here, ready for the exhibition opening," said McGurk. "Either in C & J's strong room or the bank's, next door. My guess is the bank's. So when the gun's been fired at the bank's ceiling"—he pointed the scratching stick at the bedroom ceiling again—"and everyone's on the floor, Robinson's next command will be to Mr. Braff. 'You! On your feet and take me to the strong room! And make it snappy!'"

"How—how early in the morning do you want us to be here, McGurk?" asked Willie.

"Eight o'clock should do it," he said. "But not a minute later, okay?"

21

Joey Takes Charge

I think I got only one hour's sleep that night. In fact it was still only seven fifty when Willie and I reached McGurk's house, and I wasn't surprised to see Wanda and Mari already ringing the doorbell.

"What's going on?" said Mrs. McGurk, when she opened up. "You're usually not here until nine and he hasn't even—"

"That's okay, Mom!" yelled a voice from above. "Send them up right away. *Please!*"

"Oh, go on then," she said. "And since you're all here"—by now Brains was coming up the driveway—"maybe you can see what he wants for breakfast and take it to him."

"Sure, no problem," said Wanda, heading for the stairs.

There'd been so much pent-up urgency in McGurk's voice that we felt sure something very important must have happened.

And boy, were we right!

McGurk's face was almost as white as his plaster cast, with that same grave, shook-up expression it had worn when he'd first seen the "old lady" remove the wig.

"What's happened, McGurk?" asked Wanda. "Has the wheelchair guy left already?"

"I just don't know," he said. "I didn't notice any unusual movements last night—even though I managed to stay awake until just after eleven. But—"

He was staring out of the window with that strained, agonized expression still on his face. Not staring directly across toward the Mayroyd house though, but more to the left, toward the Braff driveway.

"Go *on*, McGurk!" said Wanda. "But *what*?"

He swallowed. "Men—people—I think I might have gotten it wrong!"

"*Huh?*" Such a confession coming from McGurk was little short of earthshaking. "Why? Whatever's happened?" said Wanda.

"Because—well—just over half an hour ago, I saw Mr. Braff leave in his car. Earlier than usual. And guess who was with him?"

"Nita?"

"No. Mr. and Mrs. Robinson. They'd all come out of the Braff house together. I mean"—a look of sheer agony twitched across his face—"it seems like they *could* be treasury agents after all. And *this* was their big move. A dawn raid and the arrest of Mr. Braff!"

"Arrest?" I gasped.

"It looked like it," said McGurk miserably. "He certainly seemed very anxious."

"In handcuffs?" said Willie.

"No. He was driving. Probably just helping them in their inquiries at that stage. Taking them to the bank to check on the books."

"What about Mrs. Braff?" asked Mari.

"No sign. No sign of any of the family. Not Nita, not Dave."

"Dave's car's still there," murmured Brains, nodding toward the gray Chevy parked on the street.

"Oh, he'll be in bed at this time anyway," said Wanda. "He'll have been hanging out with my brother Ed and the other guys till the early hours. Like most nights."

"Yeah," grunted McGurk. He frowned. "But that's what's been bugging me. You'd think his father's arrest would have gotten him out of bed."

We were still gazing at the house, with its drapes still drawn, looking deserted, when someone came out of the side door and walked briskly down the driveway—a tall, beefy guy in a business suit, carrying a briefcase.

"A lawyer?" I said. "There to make sure Mr. Braff's rights haven't been violated?"

"He would have gone with them, surely?" said Mari.

Then something like a small explosion erupted, as McGurk thumped the rug with his left crutch. "*No, men!* Look at that bald head!"

"Yeah!" growled Willie. "And that cheroot he's just lifting to his mouth. It—it's the wheelchair guy! Heading back to the Mayroyd house!"

Willie was right. It *was* the wheelchair guy and he

did turn into the Mayroyd driveway. And about fifteen seconds later, with a great screech of brakes, he reappeared at the wheel of the station wagon and went speeding away down Sycamore.

Personally, I was still thinking treasury agents, that the third agent, the wheelchair guy, must have been left behind to search for additional evidence, and he'd now found it. It was probably in that briefcase. Forged bank books, stolen bonds. Maybe even Brains's college fund papers.

But McGurk was back once more with his original theory—almost.

"Treasury agents, my foot! I was right the first time!" He was still looking shaken, but now there was a very positive gleam in his eyes. Grim, but positive. "They've just been smarter than I thought. They're not going to risk holding up the bank, even with only one or two customers around. They're striking *before* it opens. With only Mr. Braff to deal with!"

"But what about Mrs. Braff and Nita and Dave?" asked Wanda. She'd suddenly gone very pale.

McGurk was already addressing Mari.

"Officer Yoshimura, phone the Braff house immediately! Let me know who answers. Pay special attention to their tone of voice!"

His knuckles were white as he gripped his crutches and Mari kept redialing. She looked worried.

"No reply, Chief McGurk. Nothing. It seems out of order. Dead."

At the word "dead" McGurk thumped the rug again.

"Right, people! Get across there now. Approach with caution, but take a peek in every window. See if you can see or hear anything."

We went. We approached cautiously. We saw nothing. The drapes were all closely drawn. But we did *hear* something. We were just about to leave, when Mari said, "Hush, please! What is that?"

Her ear was pressed to the side door. Almost instantly four more ears joined hers, glued to that door like moths attracted to light.

I heard a dull, slow thudding. Then the sound of a strangled voice. It was like someone trying to say "elf" through a wad of cotton.

And that's very nearly what it was, except the word was—"Help!"

Wanda tried to peer through the frosted glass panel.

"I think there's someone on the hall floor!"

"Leave this to me!" I said, looking around.

The garage door had been left open, with Mrs. Braff's car still inside. But that wasn't what I was looking for. I spotted a heavy hammer on the workbench, grabbed it, snatched up a sheet of oily tarpaulin from the floor, and went back to the house door. Then I held the tarpaulin close to the pane of glass and got ready to give it a whack.

It was something that McGurk himself had always wanted to do. In fact I kind of dedicated my action to him, saying, "Stand back, men!"—just before I struck.

22

And McGurk Wraps It Up

The shattering glass made an ugly sound, but the hole was just what I'd aimed for. Quickly but carefully, I put my hand through and unlocked the door. And if McGurk could have seen me then he'd have eaten his heart out!

Because there, on the carpet at the foot of the stairs, sat Dave Braff. His hands were tied behind his back, his feet were tightly bound together, and his mouth was taped shut.

His popping eyes rolled with relief. And by now, his weren't the only eyes that were popping. Farther along the hall there was something we'd been seeing for the past week, but in very different circumstances. A wheelchair. *The* wheelchair. Untidily parked, tilted forward, obviously hurriedly abandoned.

Dave quickly put us in the picture, after we'd pulled the tape from his mouth and we began cutting his hands and feet free with Brains's Swiss Army knife. Mrs. Braff and Nita were still upstairs, securely bound and gagged, but Dave had proved to be fitter and more agile—enough to get himself down there, anyway. He'd been hoping to reach the hall phone, knock it over, and dial 911 behind his back.

He hadn't bargained for the wheelchair guy cutting the telephone cord just before he left. This, after all, had been one very well planned job.

Which is why we weren't able to call the police on the spot. And why McGurk got the consolation of phoning them himself, after I'd run across to alert him, leaving Wanda and the others to help Dave cut his mother and sister free.

"Yes! The Braff house, Sycamore Avenue. Near the intersection with East Olive. . ." McGurk's face glowed as he raised the alarm. His blood must have been surging and tingling all over his body, even down his right leg, because I'd never seen him so busy with that scratching stick. "One of my officers will be standing by the curb to flag them down." He nodded to me to do just that. "*No!*" he roared into the phone, as I moved to obey. "This is *not* a hoax! This is Jack P. McGurk of the McGurk Organization! Mr. Braff has been kidnapped and you might just manage to catch them at the Berti's shopping plaza branch of the West Milford Savings and Loan, rifling the strong room!"

Even as McGurk was passing on the information that Dave had been able to blurt out to us, one patrol car was already racing along Sycamore, sirens blaring, lights flashing.

•   •   •

But the cars they sent to the bank itself were already too late. The crooks' plans made sure of that, also.

When the wheelchair guy had heard three rings on the phone at the Braff house, it was to tell him the mission was accomplished. Also that his two partners were about to leave the bank with Mr. Braff plus a couple of suitcases stuffed with selected loot (including the Marie Antoinette clock, which *had* been locked in the strong room, ready for Saturday's exhibition). They were leaving the bank in an orderly fashion, too, just as they'd entered it, with Mr. Braff having to cooperate all along the line, scared of what the wheelchair guy might otherwise do to his family.

(And this was no idle threat. As we also found out later, that guy was very far from being a vital federal witness. He was in fact a holdup specialist and hired killer himself, wanted by the police in five states and by the FBI nationwide.)

Anyway, when the police did arrive at the bank it was to find that the Robinsons and their victim had already left in Mr. Braff's car.

"So even *then* the crooks might have gotten away with it," said McGurk later that day—this time with an audience that included Mr. and Mrs. Braff, who had come across to thank us. "And they *would* have gotten away with it, too, I bet, if I hadn't remembered about the Ford. *That* was going to be their real getaway car, not the station wagon!"

"I'm afraid I'm not quite with you," said Mrs. Braff, still in a daze.

"*I* am!" said Mr. Braff grimly. "When they drove me off to that picnic area just outside of town, and the station wagon showed up a few minutes later, *I* thought it was going to be the getaway car. And I still thought so, after they'd tied me up and gagged me and dumped me in the trunk of my own car. It was the first thing I said to Patrolman Cassidy, when he lifted me out half an hour later, and ripped the tape off my mouth. 'They've got away in an Oldsmobile station wagon,' I said. 'Very dirty, but brown, I think. I'm afraid I don't have the number—'"

"But *we* did!" said Willie. "It's—"

"But it wasn't needed anyway," said Mr. Braff. "Because that's when Patrolman Cassidy interrupted me, too. To tell me the Olds had already been found abandoned in another lonely spot nearby." He turned to McGurk. "Thank goodness you were able to give them the number and description of that second car!"

"Just routine, sir." McGurk's modest little smile didn't fool anyone. "Just another product of the observation training I insist on keeping my officers on their toes with."

And that was where the gang's elaborate plans had finally come unstuck. Long before they could reach Newark airport in the Ford and catch a late-morning flight to Miami, they themselves were caught in a highway patrol roadblock. So the perpetrators never got around to making their last-minute call before boarding the plane, alerting the police to where they could find the Braff family.

"I suppose you could say that *was* kind of considerate of them," I murmured, when Mr. Braff passed on this extra piece of information.

"*Considerate*?" said Mr. Braff. "After what they'd put us through? Why, my wife nearly died of shock when that 'old lady' leaped out of the wheelchair and shoved a sawed-off shotgun in her face, late last night! After thinking she and the Robinson woman were just a couple of neighbors who'd locked themselves out and wanted to call a twenty-four-hour locksmith! And when they let in the other guy—"

He broke off with a shudder.

"Yes! *Considerate*!" McGurk echoed, glaring at me. "The whole family could have choked on their gags already, hours before the police received any last-minute call. You'll be calling their crime a *caper* next, Officer Rockaway! Like it was just a prank!"

Mrs. Braff came to my rescue. I think the memory of her ordeal had become too much for her to handle and she was anxious to change the subject.

"But tell me," she said to McGurk, "what made you feel they were going to—uh—strike—this morning?"

McGurk's scowl cleared.

"The pattern, ma'am," he said, staring down at his

dressing gown. "And the way it suddenly changed."

"The pattern?" said Mrs. Braff, also staring at the dressing gown, with its green and yellow dragons.

I could understand why she was looking so puzzled. I personally was beginning to think McGurk had gone nuts. The pressure and excitement of the last twenty-four hours must have gotten to him in his weakened state.

Then he grinned. "Yes, the pattern, ma'am. I spent some time this morning sketching it out here." With a flick of the wrist he plucked the gown to one side and revealed some notes he'd made on his private stretch of plaster.

(We kept the fragments of the cast, after it had been removed. McGurk insisted on this, saying it was a valuable exhibit—an important historical record—like the fragments they dig up from old burial mounds. Here is the first of those fragments:)

McGurk tapped the Friday note.

"They must have decided by then they were going to do it this way. Busting into your house and holding the family as hostages, rather than sticking up the bank during office hours. And when they found out there was a vacant rental so near to where you lived, they switched to the Mayroyd house."

McGurk tapped the Saturday note and turned to Mr. Braff.

"And when they heard the run-in between you and Dave, sir, that first morning—about how you were going in to work—some of those trips were to check on your movements down at the bank."

Mr. Braff nodded, frowning. "Yes, I *was* busy down there last weekend. Taking advantage of the quieter time to go through the books and make sure everything was in order for the six-month audit. Also to make arrangements about the safekeeping of the exhibition clock."

Brains suddenly piped up. "McGurk thought you might be an embezz—"

"The Robinsons' pattern, Officer Bellingham!" growled McGurk, tapping the next entry (now on a separate fragment), which read:

MON—2 trips to Berti's, only in morning.
(a) very early (Mrs. R. only)
(b) midmorning (both).

Afternoon. More interested in lounging around patio.

"That," said McGurk, "is where the pattern started to change. After he'd blundered into our first pyramid."

"Pyramid?" said Mrs. Braff, looking bewildered.

McGurk explained what he meant, then added: "Which must have made them wonder what was going on in the neighborhood, and if maybe they'd started arousing suspicions here. Then, on Tuesday—"

He tapped his next note:

TUE—R's see Officer Rockaway making notes in coffee shop.

"When they see *that*, they begin to realize they have *definitely* been arousing suspicions. Especially when they see him talking to Dolly, the checkout clerk."

"What does *she* have to do with it?" asked Mrs. Braff.

"Because they already knew they'd aroused *her* suspicions," said McGurk.

"How?" asked Mr. Braff.

"By using the express line so often, and buying fish so early most mornings," said McGurk. "*Them*. A middle-aged couple. Looking like they'd all the time in the world. Not the regular kind of express-line customers, who're usually singles, in a hurry."

Mr. Braff frowned. "No. I meant how did they *know* she was suspicious?"

"You've seen her, sir," said McGurk. "The way she looks at people. Dolly doesn't hide her feelings. Even Officer Rockaway spotted it when he was doing that observation training before all this came up. Just turn to the note you made, Officer Rockaway, and share it with these good people."

I did that, reading out the comments I'd made in the notes I've reproduced on page 29.

"Don't think the Robinsons didn't notice her suspicious nature," said McGurk. "Crooks are always extra cautious around people like that. So they must have decided to throw her off the trail."

"Uh—what trail—exactly?" said Mrs. Braff.

"Well, first, ma'am, let's just look at what they were *really* doing. They bought fish early every day, so they could keep watch on the bank early every day. They kept watch on it at that time to see how many people were around, and if and when there were ever any special deliveries, like from Brinks or other security trucks—or even when the mail arrived. And that was because that was the time they were going to strike—before the bank was officially open. Either then or when it wasn't open at all to the public, like on Saturday or Sunday."

"Go on," said Mr. Braff. "So how did they aim to throw Dolly off the trail?"

"By making notes not just in the coffee shop—which

has a good view of the bank *and* the drive-in area—but all over the store *at all times* of the day. Especially in the aisles near her checkout desk. So it would look like they were doing market research. Or even spying on the staff for the management."

"Which is exactly what she *did* think," I said.

"Very clever!" said Brains.

"The fiends!" gasped Mrs. Braff.

"Correct!" said McGurk. "Fiendishly clever, the Robinsons. But not clever enough to fool *me*."

"Us!" corrected Wanda.

"Yeah, not clever enough to fool us," agreed McGurk, passing on hurriedly to the next note on his plaster.

TUE—afternoon. Crooks getting really worried about how much we know.

"We found that out from Mr. Jones," said McGurk. "After his run-in with Robinson. So—" He tapped the end of the Tuesday note.

They don't go to plaza at all that afternoon.

"Too busy arranging for their new car," murmured Willie.

"You could be dead right, Officer Sandowsky!" said McGurk, passing on to the next note:

WED morning—Station wagon in plaza, but no Robinsons.

"They're busy trying out the new car," I said.

"Yeah," said McGurk. "Planning getaway routes and car switch locations. And *then*—" he tapped his leg again— "another major incident."

WED NIGHT/THU MORNING—Officer Bellingham's alarm system wakes neighborhood.

"And that's when alarm bells begin to ring out loud and clear in the Robinsons' heads. Forcing them to think of moving up their timetable and have Robinson himself risk paying us a visit."

THU AFTERNOON—R. pays us a visit.

McGurk had decorated this note with a string of skulls and crossbones. He added another even as we watched.

"Thankfully, I hadn't started making these notes yet," he said, blacking in the eyes of this latest skull. "But something he saw or heard on that visit must have made him decide to make his move before it was too late."

"Yeah!" murmured Wanda. "Something like Fiona

Baines Irwin's initials on your leg. Badly disguised!"

"Excuse me?" Mrs. Braff's eyes had widened.

"The FBI phone numbers," I explained.

"Whatever!" said McGurk. "The fact is that after the visit, they did make their move. But fast!"

"And we know the rest," said Mr. Braff grimly.

"Don't we ever!" said Mrs. Braff, with a shudder.

"But it all turned out okay in the end," said McGurk soothingly, with a smirk that said as loudly as if he'd had Brains record it on tape and broadcast it full volume from the top of the crab tree, "THANKS TO THE McGURK ORGANIZATION!!!"

A few seconds later his smirk vanished when Mr. Braff remembered something and said, "That last-minute call wasn't going to be made to the police direct, by the way. Robinson was intending to make it to *you*, personally."

"To *me*, sir?" said McGurk.

"Yes," said Mr. Braff. "Lieutenant Kaspar told me. He says Robinson's exact words were, 'We intended to call that brat with the broken leg who's a sight too nosy for his own good!' "

"Huh!" grunted McGurk, scowling. "Brat!" Once again his face brightened and a proud grin replaced the scowl. "*Some* brat! Even with a broken leg, we were too much for those creeps! Right, people?"

I guess that must have sounded somewhat mixed up to Mr. and Mrs. Braff—McGurk saying "*we* were too